"Uh." Luke stood there like an idiot.

"I'm Luke Anderson. Your mom wanted some landscaping work done?"

The goddess in blue jeans nodded but still didn't open the door. "Yeah, she mentioned something about that. I'll give her a call to see what's going on."

She left him on the porch, just like a smart city girl should.

She came back a few minutes later with a phone to her ear.

"Well, he's here now."

She rolled her eyes at him.

She listened for a few minutes and then said, "Fine," before disconnecting. She didn't seem happy about it, but she opened the door and let him in.

"You're Luke? From Blue Lake?"

He nodded, hardly hearing what she said because her voice so low and sweet caught and held him.

"I'm Chloe. We have a cottage there. I love your summers."

"It's a great little town." The only thing missing: a woman just like Chloe.

Chloe nodded.

He gazed down at her bare feet. Her toenails were painted a light shade of pink, each toe perfect, like a little pearl.

"So you're staying with us?"

The business person in Luke stepped out to take the place of the love-struck teenager. "I need to write up an estimate, and if she's cool with that, I'll get the job done."

"Oh, she'll be cool with

Praise for Cynthia Harrison

"Cindy Harrison's new novel, *LUKE'S #1 RULE*, again well displays her talent for taking ordinary people and events and spinning them into a tale that holds the reader tightly engaged without excess or trickery. You will quickly make friends with her characters and cheer them on to a satisfying but real-world conclusion."

~Bob Baker, author

~*~

"Cindy Harrison's newest book *LUKE'S #1 RULE* is an engrossing tale about what happens when a confirmed bachelor meets a beautiful woman with seriously inconvenient baggage: kids. Engaging, fun, and thought-provoking without guile or melodrama; real-world folks dealing with real-world problems."

~Phillips T. Chene, author

~*~

"*LUKE'S #1 RULE*, by Cynthia Harrison, is an engaging novel that shows how broken hearts can be mended, how love sometimes has to break the rules, and how seemingly hopeless situations can bloom with grace and joy. The characters are real people with real problems, yet manage to find their way to the basic goodness within. You'll love Luke and the two little boys who change his life."

~Veronica Dale, author

12/13/14

To Vernie –

Thanks for the HEA.

And everything :)

xx

Luke's #1 Rule

by

Cynthia Harrison

Cynthia Harrison

Blue Lake Series

Luke's #1 Rule

Cover Art by *Angela Anderson*

The Wild Rose Press, Inc.
PO Box 708
Adams Basin, NY 14410-0708
Visit us at www.thewildrosepress.com

Publishing History
First Mainstream General Edition, 2014
Print ISBN 978-1-62830-588-0
Digital ISBN 978-1-62830-689-7

Blue Lake Series
Published in the United States of America

Dedication

To my very own blended family,
especially my sons Mike and Tim,
who in no way resemble their fictional counterparts.

Chapter One

"I need you to stay."

Chloe Richards pushed back a wave of irritation. She wanted to snap at Rob, but since he signed her paychecks, she silently counted to ten instead.

"I'm leaving," she said, edging toward the elevator. She pulled her phone from her coat pocket to check the time. If she didn't leave right now, the boys would eat dinner without her.

"Just this once, would it kill you to share a meal with clients?"

"We had a deal." Her contract clearly spelled it out: she found the clients, put the IT teams together, and planned the programs, but she left the office every day in time to have dinner with Josh and Tommy.

After she belted her jacket a little more tightly than necessary, she pushed the elevator button and nodded toward the conference room. "We're done in there. The only thing you need to do now is enjoy your evening. I'll be back in the morning."

The elevator door opened, and she stepped inside. Rob grabbed the door, forcing it to stay open.

"I don't like fielding questions about the system without you there to answer the technical stuff." He was a large man, but he whined like a small child when he didn't get his way. Luckily, she knew how to deal with little boys.

"Talking points on index cards in your inner suit pocket." She had written out those cards for Rob; she'd seen him stick them in his pocket. If he hadn't studied them, that was his problem. She forced herself not to check the time on her phone again. "The reservation is for seven, and if you leave now, you might make it downtown on time." Rob stubbornly held the elevator door. If he didn't let go in thirty seconds, she'd personally peel his fingers from the cold steel.

"How am I supposed to explain a system I don't understand?"

"Your job is not training. Your job is projecting confidence, prestige, and success."

The client flow from the conference room had begun. Rob plastered a fake smile on his face and swept his arm toward the elevator, inviting them in. Chloe, squeezed between suits, was relieved that at least she was headed in the right direction. Still, Rob's stalling tactics rankled.

As the elevator stopped, the clients made their way outside to the waiting town car. She headed to the parking garage at the back of the building, but Rob grabbed her arm. "Just give me the short version of what the hell is going on." When she tried to jerk her arm away, he leaned in and tightened his grip. It hurt. A lot. But she would not give him the satisfaction of showing it.

She stared at Rob's hand on her arm. They were still in the lobby, and she didn't want to make a scene, so she spoke quietly. "Let go." Rob released her arm, shoving her away in the process. She caught herself before she stumbled and fell. He glanced toward the limo, then back at her.

"You disappoint me, Chloe."

This time she didn't try to hide her bad attitude. "You own this company. It's in your best interest to make the clients feel comfortable about the quality of our people. You don't have to think. We do it for you." So she was a little irate. Paying him back for the manhandling he'd just given her. Chloe turned toward the back hallway that led to the parking garage. It took every bit of self-control she could muster not to tell Rob to take a fast train to hell.

****

Beer in one hand, Luke Anderson sat with his dad, watching the Detroit Tigers play the last inning of their opening day game against Boston. At the bottom of the ninth, Boston needed to score two runs to tie the Tigers.

"Come on," his dad said to the relief pitcher. "Wipe the floor with them already." As if on command, Boston hit into a double play, and the Tigers won their season opener. Luke and his dad hit high fives. His dad yelled "Woot!" which brought his mother out from the kitchen. He really hoped she wouldn't ask him about that job downstate again.

"Good. We can eat now," she said.

Luke could smell the garlic and tomatoes in his mom's pasta sauce. He looked forward to this weekly home-cooked meal. He didn't do dinner much at his place. The occasional steak on his grill was about all he could manage. That and open a can of green beans. So he really enjoyed the food, at least until his mother started in on the downstate job again.

"My friend, Ursula, she's one of the summer people, but she's moving to Blue Lake. She needs so much yard work done on her winter home before she can sell it and move permanently up here. And then of course she'll use you for lawn and snow removal once she's a full-time resident."

Luke swiped at the last of his sauce with a bite of garlic bread and chewed. He hated saying no to his mom, but by the time he swallowed, he'd pulled his resolve together. "No." He got up from the table and bent to kiss her cheek. "Sorry."

"What? You're not staying for cake? I made chocolate. Your favorite. And I was going to pack up the leftovers for you."

He stood in the kitchen while the conflict played out in his head. If he stayed, she'd probably bring up Ursula again. But she'd probably pack up an extra piece of cake for him to take home, too. He sat.

Luke watched his mother cut the cake. Nice thick slices. Across the table, his father cleared his throat. Oh no. His father was in on it, too?

"Son, a week's wages downstate is nothing to turn down without even taking a look at it."

Luke's mom set a large piece of cake before him. He wasn't hungry for it anymore.

"I just wish I knew why you are so set on not going." His mom said this sadly, before biting into her own slice of cake.

He didn't want to go downstate because he liked it here in Blue Lake. He had his business. His house. His friends. He kept busy. Not so busy right this minute, but soon mud season would be over and he'd be rich with work again. The way he liked it.

"I planned to use this week to do some repairs on my house." An extremely lame excuse, as both his parents knew. He'd lived in the house for two years and had done nothing to enhance its bare bones. He had not even painted over the pink bathroom. He had almost no furniture, and he'd never thrown a party because he didn't really have dishes or wine glasses or chairs for people to sit in. He saw his pals at Eddie's on Friday nights, all of it good enough for him.

"What do you think of the new flat screen?" His dad seemed to change the subject, but Luke knew it for what it was. A tactic.

"Nice. I might get myself one." He had the money. His parents might think he needed the work, but he didn't. He heaved a sigh and said, "I think Abby lives down near Sterling Pines."

Nobody said anything for a minute.

Luke took a bite of cake. It cheered him instantly. And he knew his folks would stop bugging him after he admitted why he did not want to travel two hours south.

"Abby and Bella moved to Ohio last Christmas. Abby's getting married. I didn't want to tell you." Mom looked upset; Dad shook his head in disgust.

"It's already been more than two years. You have to accept the situation. Bella is not your child. She's gone. And good riddance to Abby. I never liked her."

His parents had doted on his girlfriend and her sweet little daughter. They'd all hoped for a wedding that had never happened. When Luke popped the question, Abby had dropped her bomb. She'd met someone else. She wanted him to move out of the condo.

At first he'd tried to see Bella, but Abby didn't think it was a good idea. And one summer day he'd shown up and the condo sat empty. For sale. But his dad was right. Long ago. He had to put his past behind him, where it belonged.

"Okay," Luke finally said. "I'll check out the job downstate."

****

Chloe propped herself on a twin bed, one arm around each boy on either side. Josh held the book and Tommy turned the pages, so she had both hands free to snuggle them close. Tommy's eyes closed before they finished the last chapter in *The Mouse and the Motorcycle*, but Josh took over the page and turned it without missing a beat.

When they finished, she gave Josh a squeeze before picking up Tommy for the short trip to his own bed on the other side of the night table. She tucked her little guy in, kissed him, and then turned to Josh, who watched her every move through sleepy eyes.

"Love you, honey, sleep tight." She pulled his blanket up under Josh's chin the way he liked it and kissed him goodnight.

After standing at their bedroom door for a minute drinking in the still life of her two sons at rest, she went into the kitchen to pack lunches for the next morning.

Her mother already stood at the kitchen counter slathering jam onto bread. Chloe pulled a couple of apples out of the fridge and washed them at the sink.

"I'm taking the job in Seattle," Chloe said, turning off the faucet and drying the apples with a fresh towel. Today had been the first time Rob had ever gotten physical with her, but his discontent with her need for family time had been escalating for months.

Her mother sucked in a deep breath. "Is this because I'm selling the house and moving to the cottage?"

"No, Mom. Of course not." It was partly that. She'd felt abandoned when her mom had first told her. But now, it made things easier, her conscience lighter. "It's my job. That's all this is about."

"What will Spence say?"

Chloe shrugged. Her ex had remarried, had a baby on the way, and was totally immersed in his new life. She liked Spence's wife, Bettina. She was sorry Bettina had to put up with Spence, but Chloe deserved a new life, too. She'd been living with her mom for four years, saving every penny she could. She had many, many pennies. And while her mom had been supportive and helpful, especially with the boys, it was time for everyone to move on. This had always been part of the plan.

"When will you tell the boys?"

"I'm going to wait until summer vacation." Every day she grew more confident that the next move for her family meant accepting the position in Seattle.

"If this is about money—"

"It's not." It was. Chloe didn't want her mom offering to give her the house again. She lived on a fixed income and needed the profit from the house as a cushion for her golden years. "I just need to stand on my own now. It's time."

The Seattle position paid enough for her to offer Stoner Spence a deal he would be unlikely to refuse. It paid enough for her to set up college funds for the boys. It paid enough for her to hire a nanny. Enough for a nice house in a good neighborhood with excellent schools, even at Seattle prices.

They finished making lunches in silence, but Chloe felt her mother's disappointment and disapproval anyway. If her mother knew half of the stuff Spence was into, she'd call child services. Which is why Chloe didn't tell her mom. Spence had been to rehab for pain pills and alcohol and straightened out for a while, but he'd been backsliding since the marijuana laws loosened. He said the herb calmed him. He even claimed he had a prescription for it. He smoked it in a pipe like Sherlock Holmes. Never around the boys, he promised. But she could smell the bud on his breath every time she got within an arm's length of him.

Chloe was not opposed to pot smoking. She'd been to college. She'd experimented but didn't like how it made her feel, the opposite of calm. So, sure, let Spence smoke his days away while his women support him. But not around her children. And Bettina, who Chloe loved and trusted because she loved Chloe's boys, promised that Spence never smoked around the children.

"I've got someone coming over tomorrow to cut down that old tree in back," Ursula said. "He's going to replace the fence, too. He's going to bunk in the basement for a week."

"A strange man is coming to stay here for a week?"

"He's not a strange man. He's Luke. My friend Wanda's son. Has his own business in Blue Lake."

Chloe nodded. She knew Wanda. She'd never met the son, but Wanda would have raised him right. And Mom's house needed work to get it up to code.

"I always wanted you and the boys to have this house, Chloe."

"Mom, please. I have been saving money for four years. I'm set. Honestly." Her mom didn't know she still paid the mortgage on Spence's house. "Sell your house and use some of the money to go to Hawaii."

Her mom silently wiped bread crumbs from the countertop.

"Or go crazy at the casino." That suggestion received a reluctant chuckle.

****

Luke threw some work clothes in a duffle, loaded tools into his truck, and struck out for Detroit.

As he drove south, the scenery got less and less familiar. He'd never come downstate before, never had a cause to. Crazy traffic, stores everywhere. He spotted three Walmarts in a five mile stretch, with subdivisions, gas stations, and fast food places squashed in between. People actually chose to raise their children here. He pitied them.

Sterling Pines, just another cookie-cutter town. And there weren't any pines that he could see, not many trees at all except those growing in people's yards. Where were the marshlands? Where were the woods? Where was the green space? The whole picture gave him a bad feeling.

The GPS on Luke's phone found the house, an older ranch with crab grass for lawn and shaggy overgrown shrubbery. Only a few hours south of Blue Lake, the temperature warmer, the lawns greener. He walked across the grass, and it held firm, no mud here. He went around the side of the house, checking out back. Rickety deck, ancient, rusty chain-link fence, enormous poplar that had been struck by lightning. The tree bent precariously toward the back of the house. His eyes took in the old-fashioned swing set in a far corner of the yard.

There was work here for him. He went back to the

front of the house and rang the doorbell.

A goddess in blue jeans, her brown hair streaked with gold and gathered into a messy twist atop her head, answered the door. He did not expect the slam of hunger that hit his body like a blow. He tugged on the bill of his ball cap, trying to settle down. Ursula?

"Can I help you?" Venus spoke through the screen door.

He checked the address. "Are you Ursula Muscach?"

"That's my mom."

"Uh." Luke stood there like an idiot. "I'm Luke Anderson. Your mom wanted some landscaping work done?"

The goddess in blue jeans nodded but still didn't open the door. "Yeah, she mentioned something about that. I'll give her a call to see what's going on."

She left him on the porch, just like a smart city girl should.

She came back a few minutes later with a phone to her ear.

"Well, he's here now."

She rolled her eyes at him.

She listened for a few minutes and then said, "Fine," before disconnecting. She didn't seem happy about it, but she opened the door and let him in.

"You're Luke? From Blue Lake?"

He nodded, hardly hearing what she said because her voice so low and sweet caught and held him.

"I'm Chloe. We have a cottage there. I love your summers."

"It's a great little town." The only thing missing: a woman just like Chloe.

Chloe nodded.

He gazed down at her bare feet. Her toenails were painted a light shade of pink, each toe perfect, like a little pearl.

"So you're staying with us?"

The business person in Luke stepped out to take the place of the love-struck teenager. "I need to write up an estimate, and if she's cool with that, I'll get the job done."

"Oh, she'll be cool with it." Chloe's voice had an edge he didn't understand, but, hey, city girl. Who knew? He followed her from the living room into the kitchen.

"She wanted me to show you your room. It's down here."

He followed Chloe down the stairs into a knotty-pine paneled basement, a bar with a few stools at one end, a sofa under the high, tiny window, and a desk with a laptop and stacks of papers on another wall.

Chloe walked to the closed door across from the desk and threw it open. "Your bed. Shower's around the corner."

He kept a blank face so she wouldn't know his thoughts right now. "It's fine. Great. Thanks. I'll take it. No problem. Perfect." Luke babbled when he was nervous, and his feelings about what he wanted to do with Chloe in that shower she'd mentioned made him more than nervous. He hadn't felt this alive in years, and now, pow. Wow. So good to be himself again, so good to be interested in a pretty woman. Even though they were in the basement, everything seemed brighter.

And he had a feeling she got the same rush. He could swear she'd blushed at his inept and overly expressive response to her. She went over to the desk and shut the laptop. Then she piled papers on it and started back up the stairs. "I usually work down here, but I'll move everything to my room."

"I don't want to put you out," he said. Today was his lucky day, and if she lived with her mother, as she seemed to, the coming week would be his lucky week. Was she moving up to Blue Lake with her mom? How excellent would that be?

"No problem." She started up the steps. "You can help me with the desk later." It was a small desk. She came back down for the lamp and chair, and he picked up the desk and followed her upstairs. He would follow her anywhere.

"Thanks," she said, when they got to her bedroom. She pointed toward an empty corner, and he set the desk there. "I've got some work to do, so if you'll excuse me." She turned her back to him and opened her laptop.

Her curt dismissal froze him in place. He became hyper-aware of her unmade bed. The sheets were white with tiny pink flowers. A nightgown, baby blue, tangled in the blankets.

She must have noticed him not moving because she turned her head and said over her shoulder, "The garage is open. We'll park our cars on the street so you can have access. If you need a place to write up your estimate, feel free to use the kitchen table." She actually made a motion as if to shoo him from the room.

He left the room but stood in the doorway. "When will Ursula be home?"

She let out a huff of breath and turned away from the desk to face him. "You don't get it, do you?"

"What?"

"Our moms. They're summer friends. We have a cottage in Blue Lake. They plotted this. This setup. That's why my mom isn't here. They want us to be alone for a while."

As soon as she said it, he knew it was true.

Chapter Two

Chloe sat waiting for Spence in the coffee shop halfway between their houses. Late, as usual. And why? All he did was surf the web, eat junk food, and smoke pot. When he'd first lost his Realtor job back when the economy tanked, she had to build a career. Her starting salary had barely kept them in their beautiful house. The only house her boys had ever known.

Then she got the online porn bills and saw how much money Spence took out of the bank for "walking around" cash. Really? He needed three hundred dollars a week? For what? He never even tried to find other work, just slid into depression and addiction. More than one addiction. She got a raise and sent him to rehab. He came out clean, but she'd already taken the children and gone.

Apparently, she caused every damn thing that had gone wrong in his life. Fine. She'd been fed up anyway. And to this day, he still let the women in his life support him and his habits.

Speak of the stoned, Spence blew in wearing a tan trench coat she'd bought him the first year of their marriage.

"What's so important we had to meet today?" Spence ran fingers through thinning floppy hair. Surprise, he didn't smell like weed. He continued to finger his stringy hair; he wouldn't meet her eyes.

The thought of Luke's thick blonde hair flitted through her mind. Why was she thinking about Luke now? Obviously way more fun than looking at her wreck of an ex.

She pulled herself back to the present, highly unpleasant moment. Something was wrong with Spence. Did people have withdrawals from marijuana? She wasn't sure what other drugs he dabbled in. Pregnant and blissful Bettina, too loyal to tell. He picked at a piece of lint on his wrinkled shirt for five minutes or maybe an hour. True, he didn't smell like pot, but a distinctive unwashed body odor, almost as bad, wafted her way.

Maybe he'd decided to detox. Good for him. According to Bettina, since his return from the latest stint in rehab, he started the morning with a loaded bowl and went back for more all through the day. Doctor Feelgood's orders. No doubt Spence had failed to mention he had a problem with addiction. Not her problem. Codependent no more. It would be good for the kids not to have to witness their dad with his pills, pot, powder, and premium scotch.

"I've been offered a really great job." She'd taken a half day off work to get her tasks in order. She'd visited her attorney and had a new custody agreement drawn up, allowing her to leave the state with the boys.

"Really?"

Anything to do with money made Spence's ears perk. In a few months, he'd have a new baby to think about. Ironic. He and Chloe had gone to the boys' school together to talk to their teachers about the divorce. They wanted to present a united front and wanted the teachers to know that if the boys acted out in any way, they wanted to be notified. The school principal attended the meeting. Not too many months after the divorce, she'd married Spence. Bettina. Nice lady, bad taste in men.

"It's out of state." Best to put it all on the table.

"No." His first response always, just no. She waited and sure enough, after a beat he asked, "Where?"

"Seattle."

"Absolutely not. I'll never see them." He talked fast, tripping over words, still not looking at her. She noticed that old feeling, that Mom feeling, like he was doing something wrong and hiding it from her. She had to get her kids away from him.

He'd seen the boys a total of three times this year, and it was already mid-April. It killed her a little bit every time she saw their disappointed faces when he cancelled a scheduled visitation, usually at the last minute with a paper thin excuse.

"If I take this job, I'll be able to fund their college trusts on my own." Not that he'd ever put one dime in the accounts.

"What's the offer?"

"Enough." She knew he meant salary, not position. She gave him the paperwork that freed him from any financial obligation toward their sons forever with a tasty carrot thrown in. She still owned the home he and Bettina lived in. She'd continued to pay the mortgage, so the boys would have their first home. Now, if he signed the custody agreement, she'd pay off the house and transfer title to Spence and Bettina. He grabbed the papers and scanned the document quickly. Then again.

"I'll think about it," he said.

An hour later, Spence texted. He'd signed the papers and dropped them at her attorney's office. She knew he'd put owning the house, mortgage paid, deed in his name, free and clear, before the boys. She'd counted on it, even. Still, an unwanted stab of conscience made her silence it by reminding herself they'd all be better off without him. She didn't want her boys to see him slide into some sort of worse addiction. She didn't know what he'd been using before they'd met, but the more she thought about it, she knew he'd been using *something*. The addictive behavior was escalating again. A perfect time to get out of town.

****

Chloe shut her office door and phoned Kristy in Seattle. They'd met in college and remained friends even as their lives took different paths: Kristy up the corporate ladder in Seattle and Chloe raising babies in Michigan. When Chloe returned to work, her first account was an online workshop for Kristy's company. Kristy knew what a pain Rob could be, so when a position opened up at her firm, Kristy quickly offered Chloe a spot on the human resources team. It came with a VP title, and the salary and benefits forced Chloe to think about how much she could improve her children's lives if she accepted the job.

"So did he sign?" Kristy knew the story with Spence. She'd been Chloe's maid of honor in the wedding and never admitted her discomfort with Spence until the divorce.

"Yep."

"Cold bastard."

"Yeah," Chloe sighed. "I think he's got a new drug. Not sure what." He was a different man from the one she'd married, but despite his letting them down time and again, the boys adored their dad.

"What did he act like?"

"He seemed nervous and wouldn't meet my eye. He didn't smell like pot."

Kristy was as mystified as Chloe. Their idea of getting high meant a vodka martini. One.

"You going to pay for rehab again?"

"No. I just want to get away from him. Get us all away from him. Bettina can try to clean him up this time."

"Have you written a letter of resignation?"

"This morning. Haven't sent it yet."

"Like I said before, the position opens in July."

"That's fine." More than fine. Perfect. When school let out, Chloe could take the boys on their usual vacation.

"So I'll fax you the contract."

"To my home fax."

"Of course. We are going to have so much fun!"

Chloe thought about telling Kristy about the cute landscape guy that seemed to have a crush on her, but then she decided not to get into it at work. She'd call Kristy later tonight and give her all the details.

Chloe had barely put the phone down when Rob stormed into her office. His body language confirmed what she'd always suspected: he listened in on phone calls. He was too much of a control freak not to wonder why she and Kristy were talking during business hours long after they'd finished the job. She could have used her cell phone, but maybe part of her wanted him to find out this way.

"I won't be requiring two weeks' notice," he said

as she tapped the keys on her laptop, emailing him the letter of resignation she'd written that morning after Luke arrived.

****

Chloe came home to an empty house. She went to the kitchen and heard Luke and her mom through the open window. They stood in front of the old swing set the boys hardly used anymore. It had been Chloe's.

"Chloe's dad kept it in shape, but I guess I've let it go since he's been gone."

Chloe thought of her dad with a familiar pang of longing. He died just before she left Spence. At least he didn't know about Spence's chronic unemployment, his increased drinking, his pain pills, everything that led to the divorce. She missed her dad every day but was glad to have spared him all that drama. She wiped this worn record from her mind. Forget it. That was then. This is now. And Luke with the luscious hair was in her backyard, talking to her mom.

"We'll tear this down. Not a problem."

"You don't know my grandsons."

And before she could catch Luke's response, Chloe heard the unmistakable sound of school bus air brakes and went outside to say hi to the boys. She loved that she was home early to greet them right after school.

"Mom! Grandma! There's a big truck in the driveway!"

Chloe's two dynamos came barreling into the backyard, throwing backpacks on the deck and jumping on the swings, pumping their legs in a competition of who could swing higher.

"Hey Mister, is that your truck?" Josh asked.

"I know how to read!" Tommy said. You're Luke's

19

La—"

"Landscapes!" Josh pumped his legs harder in triumph.

Luke answered with a clipped yes and backed away from the swing set.

First Josh, then Tommy, jumped into the air and landed a few feet from their swings.

"Impressive, but I told you not to jump off those swings." Chloe knew they were showing off for Luke. Not that he'd noticed. She discreetly checked the yard, but he'd disappeared.

"Wanna play basketball, Mommy?" After being cooped up in the house all winter, the boys loved coming home to sunny warm days. Josh ran into the garage to find the basketball. Tommy and Chloe followed.

Luke stood at her father's workbench holding a measuring tape in one hand and a pencil in the other.

Josh found the basketball and brought it with him over to the workbench. "Wanna play horse, Mr. Luke?"

"Mommy's going to play, aren't you?" Tommy edged closer to Luke, who hadn't answered or even looked at them.

"I am." She waited for Luke to make a polite excuse. He didn't say a word but continued scribbling notations on his paper. What was his problem? All morning he had eyed her like she was a chocolate milkshake he wanted to drink straight down, and now his eyes ran right through her. "Mr. Luke has to work. He's cutting down the tree."

"We can help." Tommy still looked up at Luke, heartbreaking hope in his eyes. Tommy, the sweetest kid in the world, loved everyone. He must have got to

Luke, because the thick-haired, thick-skulled asshole from up north finally turned away from his calculations at the workbench.

"How about you stick to playing basketball, and I'll do my work?" Luke tried a weak smile to soften his words, but Chloe wasn't buying it.

"Want to see me ride my bike?" Tommy asked. Next he'd be showing an uninterested Luke his skateboard moves.

"Tommy, honey, come on, it's your turn," Chloe said. "We seem to be bothering Mr. Luke." The hoop attached to the garage peak.

"No," Luke said. He used the side door of the garage to circumvent Chloe and the boys. A minute later, Chloe heard his truck start up.

After dinner, Chloe stood at the kitchen window, doing dishes. While she worked, she watched Luke unloading fencing from his truck, stacking it in the garage. The night darkened into black, so he had all the outdoor lights on. Her mother had insisted they save him a plate of meatloaf and mashed potatoes, but he'd probably had something to eat while he'd been out. From the mountain of supplies he moved from truck to garage, he'd bought out Home Depot.

She watched Luke finish unloading the truck and close up the garage. One by one the lights out back darkened. The stairs to the basement were right there at the kitchen door, just a little landing one step down. He didn't look her way as he brought in a duffel bag and descended.

Chloe's mom called out that she'd saved him dinner.

He didn't answer, and after a few minutes they

heard the clunk in the water pipes that signaled he'd turned on the shower.

Chloe made a face.

"Why can't you be nice to him?"

"He's rude and mean. Especially to the boys," Chloe whispered, even though the boys, engrossed in a video game, paid no attention to the kitchen talk.

"He's not comfortable yet."

"That's not it. Before he knew I had kids, he practically ate me up with his eyes."

"Oh."

"Yeah. And we both know you and his mother are hatching a plot to get us together. Obviously, it's not going to work."

Any guy who couldn't love her kids was not a guy for her. Not that she'd been searching. Time enough for love when she settled in Seattle. Any man could see that her boys were adorable, easy to love, eager to please. And Luke, what a jerk.

****

After his shower, Luke put on a pair of clean jeans and a fresh shirt. He was hungry but didn't want to deal with the people in this house. He'd never been good at apologies but knew he had to make one. If not to the boys, then to Chloe. He'd been so rude to her kids. Shame washed over him. And hunger. He'd wait for everyone to go to bed and then creep upstairs to eat the meatloaf Ursula had saved for him.

He slumped on the sofa, trying not to think about anything except the job. Christ, had his mother known Chloe had kids? Before he even thought about it, he'd pulled his phone out of the pocket of his jeans and pressed the number for home.

"Hello, son. How's it going down there?"

His dad. Who had no idea what his wife had been up to. They talked about the job for a while, then his dad put his mom on.

"Honey, everything okay?"

"Yeah, I just wanted to let you know I got here safe and sound. And the woman you wanted to set me up with? She's gorgeous."

"I, um, well." His mother wasn't sure how to respond. The notorious matchmaker usually pretended she hadn't tried to fix him up and that was the end of things. "I'm glad you like her, son."

While his mother chatted about long-distance relationships, and Ursula's move upstate, Luke mentally willed his boiling blood down to a simmer. It wasn't his mother's fault.

"She's not for me, Mom."

"Really? Why's that?" She must have heard the tone in his voice, because she whispered her words. A long moment of telephone silence ensued. He'd have to say it. He was so damn disappointed he couldn't form the words.

"Luke?" His mother's voice rose a notch, but still sounded uneasy. She must not know.

"She's got kids, Mom. Not a kid, but two kids. Little guys." Luke's gut twisted saying the words. They were nice boys. Josh and Tommy. He hadn't wanted to remember their names, but he did.

"Honey, I'm sorry. I didn't think—"

"It's okay. I just don't want you to get your hopes up, that's all." He said good-bye and let the phone fall onto the sofa. He wasn't hungry anymore.

Chapter Three

Two hours of tossing and turning later, his stomach growling all the while, Luke gave in and got up. The house sounded absolutely still. He turned on the staircase light and slipped upstairs and into the kitchen, where a nightlight burned. He opened the fridge and saw his plate of meatloaf right away. He pulled it out, ripped off the plastic wrap, and took a bite without bothering to microwave the food first.

"You might want a fork for the mashed potatoes," Chloe said. She sat on the sofa in the almost-dark, holding a tea cup in one hand. In the pale light, he saw that she wore the blue nightgown he'd seen on her bed this morning. In his mind, the nightgown fell off. He almost dropped his plate.

Luke swallowed the bite of meatloaf. "Yeah," he said, opening drawers at random until he found a fork. Then he put the plate in the microwave. "Okay to nuke this plate?"

"Yep."

She sounded distant and cold. He wanted to run back down to his hole and hide. He'd acted like an idiot around those little boys today. He should apologize right now. She probably thought he'd been angry or annoyed, but that wasn't it. He'd been trying to swallow the lump of disappointment in his throat, because he'd really liked her, but Luke only had one rule for dating: No single mothers. Been there, done that, had the broken heart to prove it.

He turned around to tell Chloe he was sorry, but she'd vanished. He sat down at the kitchen table to eat his first meal since breakfast. He didn't taste a bite. And he felt bluer than Chloe's nightgown.

Then she suddenly came back and got right up in his face, wearing a blue silk robe over the nightgown. "I don't appreciate your attitude toward my children. I'll do my best to keep them out of your way, but if I ever see you dismiss them or ignore them again, I'll kick your ass all the way back to Blue Lake."

Luke heard her but as if through a veil of gauze. Because she stood in front of the light from the stove and lit from behind like that, he saw an outline of her body.

"I'm sorry." He choked out the words and wrenched his eyes back to her face where they belonged. "I never act like that. You have to believe me. It's just—"

Chloe must have noticed his wandering eyes, because she crossed her arms over her chest. Her lovely breasts. And she clearly didn't expect his response, because her mouth hung open just a little bit. Just enough so he could see her white, white teeth and pink tongue as it darted out and did a quick lick around her full lips.

"Okay, then. Fine."

She turned and stalked back to her room. She was fine, she was foxy, but he had to stick to his rule. It would save him heartbreak. Another relationship with a single mom would kill him for sure when it ended. And relationships, for him, always ended.

He made his weary way down the stairs. Almost all of his friends were married with kids of their own. Hell, some of them had been married twice and had stepkids. What was wrong with him? He must be defective in the love department.

****

Chloe hadn't slept well. Her anger at Luke's treatment of her children made her sick. Sure, he'd apologized, but still. What an ass. And now here he came, up the stairs, the clunk of his heavy construction boots exciting the boys. Men. Rob. Spence. Luke. They made her heart hate.

"Morning, Mr. Luke!" Tommy said. His smile spread over his face like butter on toast.

Josh didn't say anything, but his eyes were glued to Luke, who might have mumbled a general hello on his way to the coffee pot.

"Okay." Chloe took the empty breakfast bowls to the sink. "Wash hands, then find your backpacks. The bus will be here any minute!"

The boys took off for the bathroom, leaving her alone with Luke. Her mother took the opportunity to sleep in since Chloe didn't have a job to go to anymore. And she probably lay wide awake in bed, giving Luke and Chloe some time alone. *Not gonna work, Mom.*

Luke found a mug, filled it, and sat down at the table. Chloe ignored him, walking into the living room and kissing the boys good-bye before they ran out to the bus stop just a few doors down.

Then she turned back to Luke. She stood looking at him, her arms crossed.

"Sorry," he said, not meeting her eyes.

"Yeah, you said that last night." She wanted to rant

26

further about innocent children and tender feelings and his half-assed apology. But instead she said, "I misjudged you. I thought you were a nice person. You aren't. And that's fine. Just get your work done and go back to where you came from as soon as possible."

Then she left the room. She checked the weather on her cell. Not a drop of rain in the next week's forecast. Excellent. He'd be out of here in no time, and she could forget all about him.

****

The next morning, Chloe woke to the sounds of a buzzing saw and two excited boys, half dressed for school.

"Mommy, Luke cutted down the tree!" Tommy hopped in place as if he were on a pogo stick. "And there's a big machine pulling out the butt!"

"It's a stump, not a butt, butt-head." Josh's words were different than his actions, because he scrutinized the activity on the other side of the window as avidly as his brother. "He's making Lincoln Logs." Josh elbowed his brother out of the way.

"Mooommm! Josh hitted me!!"

"Did not."

"Did too."

The look of quiet confidence on Josh's face reminded Chloe of Spence, back in the days when she worshipped his calm serenity. She forgot it most of the time, but she had once been moonstruck crazy in love with Spence.

"My elbow slipped," Josh said.

Tommy seemed mollified by this explanation, and Chloe gave hugs and kisses and said "Good morning." After a final hug for Tommy, the saw started up again.

Josh ran over to her bedroom window and peeked out the curtain.

"Okay, Josh, let the curtain down. Both of you finish dressing. I'll be out in a minute."

They left the room, shutting the door behind them. As she threw on a pair of yoga pants and shirt, she realized how much she had missed being home with them in the morning. She followed the voices of her mom and the boys discussing Luke in the kitchen.

"Thanks, Mom," Chloe said. She scanned the back kitchen window and accepted a cup of coffee. Chloe sipped the warm brew with one hand and helped Tommy arrange his backpack with the other. Then she set down her cup and gave both boys another hug and kiss before they ran three doors down to the corner bus stop.

"Rough night?"

Before her mom even finished asking, the stump remover racket went up a notch. Chloe put her fingers in her ears. Her mom shrugged and slotted cereal bowls into the empty dishwasher.

Chloe finished her coffee and laced up her running shoes.

"How long do you think they'll be doing that?"

"No idea," her mom said. "Do you see how much sun the yard gets without that tree?"

Chloe looked. Luke, stripped down to his undershirt, was cutting logs well away from the stump remover. His hard-muscled arms threatened to tear through the cotton of his shirt. She'd never seen a man so physically fit. That must be why her tummy, like a song she heard once, filled with butterflies and moonbeams and fairy tales.

"I'm going for a run, and then I'll take my laptop to the coffee shop." Chloe popped in her ear buds.

Her mom started to say something but saw Chloe's buds in place and simply nodded.

****

After a good long run and a quick shower, Chloe dressed in jeans and a white work blouse. She needed to do laundry but hadn't wanted to go down into Luke's lair yesterday. Now she gathered clothes from her room and the boys' and carried the basket downstairs. It even smelled like Luke down here, like pine and sand and Lake Huron.

She flew back up the steps so she wouldn't run in to him, but at the top of the stairs, she peeked out the back window and saw him working some final roots out with a shovel, the logs stacked in a neat pile in front of the garage. She stood entranced by his muscular arms for a full minute until she pried herself away from the window.

****

Luke had worked fourteen hour days all week, and for once, when Ursula came out of the house with a sandwich on a plate in one hand and a soda in her other, he took a break. Ursula's sandwiches were awesome.

"Good time for a break?"

"Yeah, thanks, Ursula." He sat on the picnic table now situated in the middle of the driveway. Ursula sat across from him.

"I waited today," she said.

"Hmmm?" He already had a mouth full of BLT.

"I didn't make your sandwich at noon like I usually do. I waited until I saw you had a good place to stop."

He chewed. "Thanks." She was a good mom. Kind

and thoughtful. Just like his own mother.

"Mom, can I talk to you?" Chloe called from inside the house. Ursula went in and came back out to collect his plate when he'd finished. She didn't seem happy. The distance Chloe and Luke had kept from each other had ruined the Mom plot.

"We've had good weather so far this spring," Ursula said.

"Bad winter, good spring," he said, quoting his mother, but also something he noticed in his line of work. They'd have a mild, sunny spring this year. He'd bet on it.

"Well, that works for me," she said as he drained his can of soda.

"I've got a bit of a situation," Ursula said. "No doubt you'll be able to hold down the fort. I just wanted you to know what's happening around here."

Luke didn't think he needed to know their family plans, but he didn't say anything. He might be a tiny bit curious about if Chloe had told Ursula that he'd upset her by being rude to the boys.

"I'm going up to Blue Lake this weekend," she said. "I've got some papers to sign with the bank up there, and well..." Ursula's fake smile had vanished. "The boys will be with their dad this weekend. That's not the problem."

Ursula stopped as if trying to figure out how to arrange her words. He smelled a setup. Leaving him and Chloe alone in the house.

"Tell my mom and dad I said hi," he said.

"What? Oh. Will do. But this is the thing. The boys are with their dad this weekend, and Chloe won't be around either."

He bet Chloe had smelled another plot and had foiled their mom's plans.

"Fine," he said. "I'll be fine."

"Of course you will," Ursula said. Then she walked back into the house.

Luke stood there, his work forgotten for the moment. Where was Chloe going? And why? Desperate to avoid him, no doubt. And a good thing. It would help him keep his number one rule.

It took him all day, but Luke finally pulled the last root from the ground. They'd spread from the back of the yard all the way to the house. His arms were dirty and his muscles ached, but by the place of the sun in the sky, it was still midafternoon. He decided to take a shower and have something to eat. He'd completed the tearing down, time to build back up. He'd start with the new privacy fence.

He'd cleaned up and taken another of Ursula's sandwiches to the picnic table, more out of habit than anything. He heard car doors slam out in the street—his truck parked in the driveway out front, blocking his view. Seconds after a cream-colored Cadillac streaked into view and away, the gate opened.

"Luke!" Tommy and Josh said at the same time.

"Whoa. What are you guys doing here? I thought you were going to the Tiger's game with your dad tomorrow."

"Bettina's baby hurts her tummy. Daddy gave us the tickets." Josh fanned out four tickets and then placed them back in his shirt pocket.

Okay. Obviously some sort of emergency situation. Chloe's ex hadn't even stopped long enough to make sure anybody was home.

"Where's Grandma's car? Where's Mom's car? Are you babysitting us, Luke? What are we gonna do? Should we play horse? Can you make us a snack? Or we can help you build your fence!" Tommy acted like he'd been mainlining caffeine. Kid had a boatload of energy.

Josh hadn't said anything since he'd stashed the Tigers' tickets in his pocket. He kept quiet, maybe a little too quiet.

"Snacks in the house, silly," Luke said to Tommy. He took the boy's backpack off his shoulders—the thing was bigger than the kid—and turned Tommy gently around and guided him to the kitchen door. To Josh he said, "Your mom will be here later. Grandma went away for the weekend."

He needed to call Chloe and give her the scoop. He hoped that whatever her activities she could get out of them and head home soon. He pulled his phone out of his pocket and realized he didn't know Chloe's number. He'd have to call Ursula first.

"You're babysitting?"

Josh, at eight, was more perceptive than Tommy. He'd probably sensed Luke keeping his distance. His behavior toward the boys deeply shamed Luke.

"Nah," Luke said to the babysitting question. "You're big enough to watch yourselves, right?"

Josh nodded solemnly. He seemed a little scared. It was likely these boys, between their mom and grandma, had never been left on their own for more than a minute.

Luke got Ursula on the phone with one hand while he opened the cookie jar and set it on the table with the other. She didn't ask him why he needed Chloe's cell number, and he didn't say anything about the situation. As Chloe's line rang, he pulled a liter of Coke out of the fridge. Tommy's eyes lit up. Josh opened his mouth, then shut it, like he wanted to say something. Too late, Luke figured out they probably got a healthier after-school snack than sugar layered with caffeine layered with sugar.

"I been thinking," Luke said. "If you boys are up to it, after your power snack, maybe you could help me put up that fence." It wasn't true. The guy that sold him the fence had a couple of people coming out to do the fencing. He just wanted to be nice. Tommy's sunny smile broke out over his face. He lifted his cookie in the air and did a fist pump. "Yes!"

"I'll pay you of course." Luke looked at Josh, who cautiously bit into a cookie. "Or if you don't want to help, that's cool. You can watch television or play video games."

Chloe finally answered her phone, and Luke walked into the living room. He gave her the details, omitting that Spence had dropped the kids off in the street.

"Oh, that jerk. Again! And the game tomorrow..." Chloe sounded sad, but she pulled herself together and told him she'd be there in an hour. Then she hung up without saying good-bye.

Josh had finished his cookie and stood staring out the window into the backyard.

"Looks like you don't really need our help," he said.

Luke went over to see what he was talking about. The fence guys were on the job.

"I won't lie, they do that job better than I do. But I

could use some extra hands. For the deck." Luke could put up decks in his sleep.

"What ya payin'?"

"Five bucks an hour. Each." He didn't think they'd last an hour. Holding planks in place was pretty boring work.

"Hm. Okay." Josh perked up with the swift infusion of sugar and caffeine into his system. "Mom usually makes us show her our homework."

"You can do that later."

"She wanted us to get it done today, because tomorrow…"

"We're going to the Tigers' game with Daddy!"

"No, we're not." Josh pulled four tickets from his back pocket and put them on the table. "Dad can't go."

Luke beheld the tickets. There was no more avid fan, but he'd never been to an actual game. It sucked that their dad had bailed on such a cool event.

"Mommy will take us!" Tommy said. "Right, Luke?"

"Yep. She'll be here in a little while." Should he settle them at the kitchen table with their homework? He didn't know the first thing about homework. Let's see, an eight-year-old would be in third grade. Tommy, in first grade, couldn't be too hard. But he really needed to get going on the deck. Daylight savings time hadn't kicked in yet, and he had a limited number of hours to work.

"Okay, dudes, here's the plan. Only if you want to, you can help me with the deck for an hour and then you do your homework. If you need help with homework, you can come and ask me. And your mom will be home soon." Luke hoped she'd hurry.

Chapter Four

Luke wondered how he'd gotten into this mess. Ah yes, the lure of a fat check and a couple of meddling mothers. He still didn't know what to do about the moms, but one problem at a time, or two pint-sized problems, was all he could deal with.

The boys were each on their third, or maybe fourth, cookie. He got out one more for each of them and one for himself and then put the lid back on and the jar, a clear glass container that would show Chloe exactly how many chocolate chip cookies had been consumed in her absence, back on the counter.

"Well, let me see if I have work gloves for you boys." Luke had extra gloves, but not their size. Still, it wouldn't hurt to protect their little hands. Not that the decking would splinter, it only resembled wood, but just in case. And since they wouldn't be moving much, he figured even large-sized gloves would do the job.

As he got parts and tools in order on the driveway, he thought about this deck. Who puts up a deck to sell the house? Might increase sales price. Not his house, not his decision. This could not be another romance tactic. Something to keep him here longer.

"I got a tool kit!" Tommy said, racing out to the garage, leaving him alone with Josh.

"He's such a baby. It's not real tools. Our grandpa gave it to him. The hammer is plastic."

35

Luke smiled.

"So, you gonna help us, or do homework?"

"I'll help," Josh said. They walked out into the garage. "I know where Grandma keeps the real hammer." Luke quickly tried to think up small risk-free jobs that weren't beyond the boys' capabilities.

"I need to use the bathroom first," Tommy said, hopping from foot to foot.

"And we better change into work clothes," Josh said.

A few minutes later, Tommy called out in an excited voice, "Luke, Luke. Come here, Mr. Luke."

Luke followed the voice into the house, through the living room and down the hallway into a typical boys' room, royal blue carpet and twin beds. Both boys lay on the floor next to the bed closest to the door. A white rabbit sat on the bed, black ears sticking straight up, pink eyes alert.

"Come on, Dumpster, you can do it." Josh spoke in calm tones, while Tommy yelled, "Jump, Dumpie. Jump!"

Then, to Luke's astonished eyes, the rabbit took a flying leap over both boys and landed on the floor next to them. They got up and clapped.

"Wanna see what else he can do, Luke?"

"Sure, if it doesn't take too long." Luke thought about the deck. He'd planned to have it staked before dark. Before babysitting duty. He was taking care of Chloe's kids. That fact should bother him, but it didn't. Not even a little.

"We always play with Dumpster when we come home from school. Mom says he doesn't like being away from us for so long, so we have to give him some tension."

Luke figured out Tommy's word for attention. "Well, okay, one more trick."

The boys conferred about which trick to show him.

"He can poop in a litter box, but he only does that when he has to go," Josh said.

"I know. Put him on his back!" Tommy vibrated with excitement.

Josh gently handled the rabbit, petting him on his head between his ears with two calm fingers and whispering something to the furry beast. Then he lay the rabbit down on his back. The rabbit lay there stock still, frozen in space, all of his fur and legs and arms tucked in like a yoga master. The bunny held absolutely still, seemingly floating on his spine without a care in the world.

For once, the boys were silent, too.

After a minute or two, Josh said "Okay, buddy," and the rabbit flipped over and scampered to a litter box in the corner, where he dug furiously, scattering litter across the rug.

The boys sat on the floor, legs crossed, beaming at Luke.

"That's one special bunny you boys have," Luke said.

"He's really smart. He's my bunny, but I let Josh share him," Tommy said.

"I used to have a hamster, but he died," Josh said, solemnly.

"I'm sorry." Luke began to form a dangerous rapport with this little guys.

"Yeah. He's buried under the tree in the front yard."

"We had a cross made out of Popsicle sticks, but something happened to it during the snow storm."

"I gotta get Dumpy his carrot, and then we can go help you make the fence for Grandma," Tommy said, leaving the room at his usual speed of light.

Josh cuddled the rabbit, who had hopped into his lap. Luke could actually feel each brick in the wall he'd built around his heart begin to loosen, one at a time.

****

Chloe threw clothes in her weekend bag, happy to leave the hotel a day early. She'd ordered room service, watched movies, shopped the outlet stores, bought a purse, read a book. She'd been bored out of her mind. Luke's call a welcome relief. Not because of Luke, she couldn't care less about him, but she needed to be there for her boys, whose dad had let them down. Again. She made a mental note to call Bettina, who didn't like the fact that Spence sometimes acted sixteen instead of thirty-six, either.

She drove ten over the speed limit all the way home, then went in the front door. She headed straight for her room where she dropped her laptop and kicked off her shoes. The house was quiet. Luke and the boys must be out back.

She pulled her curtain back and peeked. Her two little guys held a deck post. They had wide smiles on their faces at something Luke said as he cemented the post in place. They looked so cute in their oversized gloves. They glowed with pleasure. Her phone buzzed, and she pulled it out of her pocket.

A text from Spence. "R okay, but have to skip game. Gave J tix."

Chloe, never a fan of baseball, basketball, hockey,

or any other team sport, went along with the hoopla for the boys. The closest she got to a team sport was the occasional yoga class. But of course she'd have to take them to the game. No question. They'd been anticipating this for weeks. That jerk Spence.

"Hey." She walked into the kitchen and opened the patio door.

All three faces turned toward her.

"Hi, Mommy. We're helping Luke."

"Thanks, team, I got it from here." Luke wiggled the post a fraction, testing the hardening cement. He kept his eyes on the ground. Tommy ran up and hugged her. Although the temperature stayed a coolish 60-something or other, he radiated heat.

"We're doing a project!"

"I see that," she said. Josh joined his family at the door and Luke, finally satisfied with the cement, came over to where Chloe stood with the boys. "I hope it's okay that I put these guys to work."

"Sure. It's fine. But I think it's time for dinner now."

"Can we get pizza?" Tommy asked.

"We really worked up an appetite," Josh added.

"I'll run up to Little Tony's."

"I'll go," Luke said.

Another nice surprise. First, Luke being so sweet to the boys. Now offering to get dinner. Next, he'd be sitting down at the table with them.

When Luke returned with a large pizza, plus bread sticks and an antipasto salad, she thanked stars she'd set four places instead of three because he opened the pizza, took it out of the box, sat it right down in the center of the table, and grabbed a slice and a seat at the same time. He took his first bite before his butt hit the chair.

Chloe caught Josh watching Luke load up his salad bowl and did the same. Josh never ate salad. Chloe kept her mouth shut. Too much to hope both boys would turn into salad eaters at the same time. Tommy went right for a bread stick, dipping it in the plastic tub of accompanying sauce.

Tomato sauce counted as a vegetable, didn't it?

"Luke, Grandma got us Tiger shirts for the game tomorrow!" Tommy said.

"And she got us baseball hats with a capital orange D on them!"

Both boys were already wearing their caps. Just like Luke. Before they'd met him, they hadn't been keen on ball caps.

"Are we going with you and Luke now, Mommy? Because we didn't do our homework yet." Josh looked from Luke to Chloe.

The boys and her mom had watched every game the Tigers played since opening day back in April, and were excited with their team tied for first place in the division. They had begged to wear their orange T-shirts with the tiger leaping through the gothic navy blue D so often that they were already soft from washing.

"Yeah, Luke! You should come! They got cool rides and cotton candy and and…" Tommy shot out the words so fast Chloe didn't have a chance to slow down this plan the boys spontaneously hatched.

"Here's the tickets, Mommy." Josh pulled four bent tickets from the back pocket of his blue jeans. "And we'll do our homework right after dinner."

"Right," Tommy said, pulling a slice of pizza from

the cardboard tray and stuffing his mouth so full Chloe wasn't sure how he could chew.

"Sorry, dudes, I gotta work," Luke said.

"Aw, man. Mommy, can't Luke have a day off?"

Chloe couldn't finish the piece of pizza on her plate. Her anger at Spence warred with sadness that Luke shot the kids down. Not that she wanted his company at the game. But the boys would love it. It might take their minds off their absent father.

"It's fine," she said. She smiled so brightly she thought her face would break. "The three of us will have a great time!"

"You hate baseball," Josh said.

"Who hates baseball?" Luke asked.

Instead of answering, Chloe got up and threw the rest of her pizza away. Then she rinsed the dish. The three males at the table ate in silence for a while, but, one by one, they brought their plates to Chloe for rinsing. Luke went down to his lair. She cleared the table, and the boys brought out their homework. She sat down to help them.

After homework, Chloe let them watch Sponge Bob while she returned a call that had come in earlier from Kristy.

"Hey, Kristy. It's Chloe."

"Yeah, hi, just checking in. You home from the no-tell motel?"

"Yeah. Not as sexy as it sounds. Outlets are overrated."

"You sound funny. Everything okay?"

Chloe told Kristy about Spence's latest stunt.

"So the hunky landscaper isn't a sports fan?"

"I think he kinda is," Chloe said. Then she changed

the subject and asked Kristy if she'd chosen her wedding gown yet. The wedding, more than a year away, yet super-organized Kristy already checked things off her to-do list.

"Yes. I feel like a princess."

Chloe remembered the feeling well from her own wedding. She smiled, realized Kristy couldn't see her, forced out a lame chuckle. Then she sighed.

"You've got a crush, girl."

"Who, me? No. It's not that."

But her traitor heart had gone soft watching the boys and Luke work together. She owed him big for babysitting duty. And being so nice to her sons. A huge improvement over loser Spence.

Chapter Five

Spence texted Chloe. He felt terrible for lying, for using Bettina as an excuse for his own purposes. He'd taken a pill the minute they left, but it took awhile for pills to work, so he got out the whiskey and poured a straight one, drinking the entire glass in one long continuous chug. Still, his mind wouldn't get off the guilt train. He was a bad dad. But it wasn't his fault. He hated being a part-time zoo daddy. Chloe didn't realize that he skipped so much visitation because it hurt too much to be with them for a short time and then let them go. Easier just not to see them. No, it wasn't. Nothing easy about this. And he saw no way it would ever get better. He loved them, but they'd be better off without him. And he had to figure out how to be a better dad to not only Josh and Tommy, but to his new child, too.

He was "less than" in every way, not just as a dad, but as a husband, as an expectant father, as a wage earner, as a human. Lowest of the low. God, when he got like this only smoking his pipe helped. He poured another drink and went down to the basement, which is where Bettina insisted he smoke. Like a teenager hiding from mom. His brain didn't stop: lazy, living off his wife, pot-head, deadbeat, no will power. Subhuman. Until he lit his pipe. The pill kicked in, too. And the whiskey put a pretty sheen over all his problems.

By the time Bettina returned from her errands, he

lay prone, ensconced on the sofa, his favorite pillow under his head, content in the moment of his pleasant buzz.

Bettina could always tell when he was high. He knew she didn't like it, but she put up with it. Until today. "Spence, you have to promise me you'll stop smoking pot when the baby comes."

"I have a prescription!" Fake, but she didn't need to know that.

"I saw an empty whiskey bottle in the kitchen. So thoughtful of you to leave it out for recycling."

Women could be such buzz kills. He needed another pill, the ones that put him to sleep. He tried to rise from the sofa and got dizzy, falling back down, half on the cushions and half on the floor.

"Oh God. Listen to me. You are not in any shape to care for an infant. Your drug use, the alcohol, it's escalating. Why? Are you anxious about the baby? Because I sure am." As she spoke, she helped him sit up.

"I feel like shit."

"You should. You're missing the game with your boys."

"I can't handle it."

"What about them? Do you even care? Do you want to see them before they move out of the state? Why would you let Chloe take them away?"

He heard her words, but the questions got mixed up in his mind. "I'll be right back," he said. He propped himself up and walked upstairs to his office. Where he used to work. Where he'd sold million dollar houses. The walls were full of plaques and citations for his selling. All that gone now. Now he worked on staying alive another day. He found the right pill and gulped it down without water.

Bettina had followed him upstairs. "You stink." She stood in the doorway, blocking his exit.

"So I'll shower. Then I need to go to bed. You have no idea what I'm going through."

"Like hell I don't. I'm going through it too, and it's breaking my heart, damn you."

He stumbled into the shower and stood under the water for a few minutes. He picked up the soap and immediately dropped it. He turned off the water and went to bed without even drying himself off.

Bettina feared Spence's addictions were roaring back. Worse, she had begun to think of the baby as *hers*, not *theirs*. That scared her the most. Distancing herself from Spence in case Chloe had been right about him all along.

Spence snored, passed out cold as she searched online for an Al-Anon meeting. These, Chloe had told her, were for spouses and families of addicts. That's who she had become. She had to face it. Denial doesn't just affect addicts. It runs in their families, too. Spence didn't seem to have any friends, and she had, without even realizing it, distanced herself from friends and coworkers so she would not have to be embarrassed when Spence had "one too many."

While the search engine ran, she rubbed her belly and looked out the window. Just twilight, and her husband out for the night, nothing like a family dinner even dimly in view. She sighed; she'd heard that even inside the womb, a baby could sense its mother's distress. It impacted the child, made them more prone to anxiety. Well, that was one theory. She closed her eyes and breathed deeply. She hoped that study proved wrong, but she had to stay as calm as possible just in case.

She seemed to be making a lot of "just in case" plans. That scared her, too. She scrolled through the hits her search brought up. Stopped at a meeting held in a nearby church. They had literature about living with an addict. Better yet, they had an open meeting in thirty minutes. Spence would not even know she'd gone.

She got up from the chair slowly, her hand on her back, which seemed to be chronically cramped these days. She locked the door on her way out of the house even though a part of her that wished someone would come and steal her husband. That would solve all her problems.

The drive to the church meeting made her feel lonelier. It wasn't a religious meeting. There was no prayer she had left unsaid. Spence's demons were his own, nothing to do with her. She knew that much going in. This meeting consisted of a simple nuts and bolts approach to dealing with an addict. How to stop enabling. Had she been doing that? What was it, exactly? She parked her car, walked toward the church, every step filled with anxiety and guilt. If she was an enabler, then the things happening with Spence were partly her fault, right?

She scanned for the right room. Only one of several classrooms had lights on. She looked in the door. The participants—mostly women—sat in a circle. They were people like her. People who lived with addicts. She was the only pregnant one. She picked out a low-risk spot and lowered herself into a chair between two women who seemed the most nonthreatening.

"We are not here to judge," said a guy from the crowd, moving to the front of the room. "We are here to help you detach from those negative feelings."

Damn, she should write that down. She hadn't brought her notebook. So not like her to be unprepared. She opened her purse and ruffled through its contents, coming up with a pen and the empty back of a pink message slip from one of her teachers.

Meanwhile, she'd missed what the guy had said about detaching, so she just wrote down the word "detach." He went over some rules, first names only, like an AA meeting in a movie of the week. Nobody made her talk. She just needed answers. She didn't want to explain. Her bones ached and her mind melted. Nobody told you how pregnancy made your body so tired. She could almost take a nap, sitting up in this deeply uncomfortable metal folding chair.

The guy in front had stopped talking and now the woman next to her spoke in a soft voice. She told a story about being so disconnected, distracted by five children, that she had not known how deep her husband had fallen into addiction until he didn't come home for two days.

She called the police, but they were inclined to wait and see. They knew his name. He'd had a drunk and disorderly. A DUI. Sure, they'd keep an eye out, but Detroit was in bankruptcy, or hadn't she heard?

Bettina wanted to reach out and hold the woman's hand, her voice trembled so. "He came home minus two fingers. He'd fallen asleep in a crack house, and rats ate them while he was in a heroin stupor."

Bettina shivered. Spence wasn't as bad as all that. He had never had a DUI or got arrested for being drunk and obnoxious. Of course, he mostly stayed home these days. Maybe she was in denial. Her head pounded. She tried to listen to the guy in front talk about depersonalizing the situation. Really? Your husband has his fingers gnawed off by rats, and you don't take it personally?

She wrote down the word "depersonalize" anyway. But the image of those bloody fingers would not leave her brain, so she didn't catch how exactly you were supposed to depersonalize. The meeting broke up and she went out to her car.

She saw the lady who'd sat next to her and told the awful story.

"You are so brave," Bettina said.

"I'm a work in progress." The woman smiled. "I'm Suzy." She held out her hand.

"I'm Bettina."

"I hope you'll be back."

"I don't know…"

"Listen, you want to grab a cup of coffee?" Suzy checked Bettina's belly. "Decaf?"

Bettina battled inside. She didn't talk about Spence's problems to anyone except Chloe. Maybe that wasn't healthy, seeing as how his ex-wife would not be exactly impartial.

"Okay. Maybe some juice."

"Meet me at the family restaurant, the one of the next corner south of here?"

"Yep. I know the one. See you there." Bettina had never actually been in this restaurant, because it did not serve alcohol, and when Spence began his moderation program, he always liked his beer with dinner out. She wished she would have made up an excuse not to meet

Suzy. She just wanted to go home. No, not really. She didn't want to go home. She just didn't want to talk to anyone. Lonely but also uninclined to share. It was messing with her head. And the baby. She took one hand from the steering wheel and patted her tummy.

After they got a booth, Bettina found it easier to talk than she could have predicted. "So, five kids?"

"Yep."

"How does that make them feel, their dad's fingers?"

Suzy's face blanked as she searched for the right words. "We didn't tell them the truth. We said he got hurt on the job and was in the hospital for a few days."

"Oh. Is that one of the tactics that guy talked about tonight? Detaching?"

"No. I suck at all of the techniques. I'm keeping my kids in a toxic environment, and I'm lying to them. I'm enabling, and I'm teaching them denial. And how to lie." Suzy's nose wrinkled and her eyes stole skyward; Bettina's face did the same thing when she tried to hold back tears.

"Have you been coming to these meetings long?"

"Two years. Ever since he hurt his back and got hooked on pain pills."

"I'm sorry."

Suzy shook her head. A small smile crossed her face and disappeared. "Thanks. We're in this together."

"So the finger thing. That didn't make him stop?"

"Hell no, it's the shiny new excuse for why he can't stop. He feels so sorry for himself he shoots up at home now." Suzy seemed surprised by the venom in her voice. She sighed. "Sorry. I am just so fed up. But my oldest kid is ten. I have nowhere to turn, no one will want a woman with five kids, not her own sister, or her brother, not even her mother.

"Listen, hon, I wanted to give you some advice. Off the books."

Bettina did not want advice from someone who would stay with a man who continued drugging after being eaten by rats, but she listened anyway. What should she do, get up and walk out? Say, "this is where I draw the line"?

"This one your first?" Suzy nodded her head toward Bettina's belly.

"Uh-huh. Two stepsons. Sweet boys. Mom has full custody."

"That's a blessing."

Bettina wondered if that was true. Spence had gotten worse since he'd given up his rights to the kids. Or possibly she was in denial again, or making excuses for him, just like Suzy did for staying with her husband.

Suzy leaned in close so nobody could hear her. "Get out."

At first Bettina misunderstood and thought she'd upset Suzy. She thought Suzy told her to leave the booth before her herbal tea even came. Just then the waitress brought the tea. Suzy had a huge Diet Coke and a jelly donut. It looked really good, but Bettina knew she'd have indigestion and heartburn all night if she had one.

The waitress left, and Suzy bit into her donut with gusto. She chewed and talked at the same time. "Get out while you can, hon. One kid? That's a snap. You work?"

Bettina nodded.

"Well, there you go. Got a mother who will watch

the little one?"

"My folks live in Arizona. Retired. My husband was supposed to watch the baby. He wasn't this bad when I first got pregnant. I thought he'd get better, but he's just gotten worse."

"Hell, honey, will they take you in, in Arizona?"

"Probably." Bettina, proud of her independence and her work, didn't want a repeat of Chloe's life. Back home to mommy.

Bettina finished her tea, and Suzy sucked down her Diet Coke. She held up her plastic cup for the server to refill. "I've got to go. I'm dead on my feet." Blame the pregnancy. Lie. A white lie. A kind lie. She and Suzy would never be friends, and she was never going to go back to that meeting again. Those weren't her people. She didn't really have any people, but no people seemed better than these people, who were just as stuck as her.

Suzy nodded. "See you next week?"

Bettina nodded as she hefted her bulk from the booth. Head down, eyes into her purse, she found and set out a couple of dollar bills for her tea. She didn't want to look at Suzy and lie.

She got in her car and headed home, thinking a thousand things at once. Depersonalize. How to do that? Don't take Spence's dangerous antics personally? As in, they are not my fault? She knew that. Okay, don't be hurt by his failure as a husband and father. Hmm. Easy to say "don't be hurt" but harder to do. She pulled in her driveway, having no idea how she'd gotten there. Didn't matter. She went inside, checked the bedroom. Nothing had changed. Spence lay naked, his hair plastered to his head, snoring. She decided to sleep on one of the boys' beds. She'd picked up some literature at the meeting that she hoped would shed some light on those terms detach, depersonalize, set boundaries. She was so tired, but labeling herself the biggest loser in the world kept her awake. She set boundaries every day at work. She didn't take hurtful remarks personally, she detached and kept working. So why couldn't those same tactics work at home?

****

Luke answered his cell, glancing at the caller ID first.

"Hi, Mom."

"Luke! You cannot let her go downtown alone with those boys tomorrow!"

"What?" He knew what his mother meant. The Tigers' game. He just needed time to think of a way to get her off his back.

"They call Detroit the Murder City."

"That was years ago."

"Well, they still have crime: drugs, shootings, gangs."

"Not in that part of town. They'll be perfectly safe."

"But you love baseball. You've always wanted to see a game."

Luke let his mother talk, lying out on his bed to stretch his muscles. He could tell it would be a long conversation, but eventually, she'd wind down. The only person who hadn't tried to talk him into going to the game was Chloe.

"Honey," his mom said, "I know Abby hurt you horribly when she took Bella away, but let's face it, at your age, the only available women are going to likely already have a child or two."

That wasn't true. He'd only had to invoke his rule a time or two. Then he realized if he dated women ten or so years younger than himself, none of them had kids. They didn't have a lot of ambition or personality, either, most of the time, beyond buying the newest designer purse or finding a better job, anywhere but in Michigan. Or finding a husband who already had a job. He hadn't met anyone since Abby who he'd even remotely felt like he could marry. Marry. For God's sake, why had that word popped into his head? A chill ran up his spine.

As his mother chatted on, he listened to the noises from upstairs settle down. He'd bet the kids were in bed. They'd been as excited as if it were Christmas tomorrow, despite their dad bailing on them. They seemed to take the blow in stride. Ursula had mentioned that Chloe's ex wasn't always reliable when it came to seeing his boys. How could a guy with a family like Chloe, Tommy, and Josh just dump them? It didn't make any sense.

"Chloe hates sports," his mother said. "She's doing this for the boys, but it's just not her thing. She practices yoga and likes to run."

Luke wondered how anyone could dislike team sports. Most of the women he went out with loved the games. Loved going to sports bars and eating nachos and drinking beer and cheering when the Wings scored a goal or the Pistons sank a basket or the Tigers hit a home run. Hell, they cheered when somebody made it to first base.

"Luke?"

His mind had wandered.

"Sorry. I'm tired. The boys and I started on the deck today."

His mother said something he couldn't hear to someone else in the room. She must have put her hand over the phone, because the voices were muffled.

"Okay, honey, well, it's your decision," his mother said.

That surprised him. He figured she'd rattle on for another half hour of persuasion. But no. She handed the phone to his dad. Dad asked about the job, where he was with it, when he'd be getting back to Blue Lake. He asked his dad about his latest project, rebuilding an old chopper motorcycle.

The end. Conversation over and good night. Luke flipped from his right side to his left. He rearranged his pillows. His dad hadn't mentioned a word about the Tigers' game. Probably he didn't know Luke had been offered a free ticket. He and his dad always watched the games together. Even after he'd moved out to live with Abby and then in his own house, he still stopped in on game days, or his dad came over to his place.

They'd always talked about going to a game. Driving down to the city, only a couple of hours away. Maybe getting a room for the night so they could drink as much beer as they wanted and not worry. Somehow, they'd never done that.

He flipped over onto his back and stared at the ceiling. He really wanted to go to that game, damn it. He had no doubt that Chloe could take perfectly good care of herself and her sons. He knew they'd be safe. She was a big girl. She didn't need him to protect her. Neither did the boys. They were good boys, but they already had a father. A crappy one, but still.

He gave up on the idea of going to sleep, got up to pee. Then he sat down and checked his list. Finish up the deck. Two, maybe three, days. Then, lay the sod in one day and plant the shrubs in one more and he'd be out of here late next week.

It wouldn't be so difficult to miss a day of work. Even if things went wrong, which they sometimes did, he'd still be home by next Sunday, at the latest. The chance of a lifetime. Seats in right field. Close to the action. Directly in the line of his favorite player, number thirty, Dan "the hit man" Dobbs. His dad liked the new hot-shot pitcher. Well, didn't everyone? But something about Dan Dobbs, some kind of heart, made Luke root for the ball player who came up on the mean streets of Detroit to play for his home team. He wondered if Tommy and Josh had favorite players. He'd bet on Wade Straight for Tommy and Leon Ruiz for Josh. Could he really let the boys go to the game with a woman who didn't understand or enjoy the sport?

He listened for noises upstairs but heard only silence. So he went up and grabbed a Coke out of the fridge. Came back down to his lair. He wondered if the boys collected baseball cards. That had been a passion of his as a kid. His mother had given them to him a year or so ago along with a box of his childhood things. Yearbooks, stuffed toys, action figures, even an old comic book. He'd trashed everything but the baseball cards, which he kept in special plastic sleeves all tucked into cardboard boxes made specifically to hold collections.

He bet they sold a lot of memorabilia down at the ball park. He could get that stuff online if he wanted it, but seeing it, actually looking at the stuff, would be so much better. He needed a new ball cap. He could get his dad a shirt from the stadium. Father's Day would be here before you knew it. He got his tablet and searched Comerica Park for the heck of it. Checked tomorrow's lineup. Dobbs was batting second.

He heard a noise upstairs. The fridge opened. A pop can top popped. Steps coming toward his stairs.

"Luke? You up?"

"Yeah."

She started down the steps, her long legs coming into view first. She had awesome legs. Her shorts gave him the full effect. "Can't sleep?"

"I never go to bed until midnight," he said.

He had been shocked to see the time by the digital clock of his open tablet. 11:30. It seemed way later to him until she came down, working like a double shot of espresso on his energy level. She sat next to him on the old sofa. She could have sat in the desk chair, but she didn't. She sat next to him. He liked having her there. That was the problem, in a nutshell. *Remember your rule*, he warned himself.

Her eyes checked out the open page on his tablet, then widened in surprise.

"I'm just so pissed at that asshole," she said, turning away from the tablet. "Bettina had heartburn! So he drops them on you without a thought and cancels tomorrow's plans, too." She took a breath, filling her lungs and letting it whoosh out. This caused interesting things to happen beneath her T-shirt. "Thanks, by the way, for keeping an eye on them."

"No problem. They're good boys."

She nodded.

"I know you can take care of yourself," he said.

"Huh?"

He liked the way her eyes scrunched up when she got confused. "My mom. She called, wanting me to escort you and the boys to the game because it's big, bad Detroit."

Chloe laughed. "The Mom Plot continues."

"I know."

"Don't worry. I'm not in on it."

"I didn't think you were."

"Those two have no scruples when it comes to fixing us up. I mean, they figured we'd be alone in the house together all weekend."

"Where did you go?"

"Nowhere important. I just didn't feel like being manipulated by a senior citizen who's read way too many romance novels. They'll get the picture soon enough. I mean, see, already, their latest plot is falling apart. They thought we'd be alone all weekend, and we won't be. You'll be here alone, and the boys and I will be downtown all day. The game won't get over until six or seven. If they're still hungry after all the hot dogs and ice cream, we'll go out to dinner. I will keep them out of your hair. They'll be too tired and excited to bother you."

"They don't bother me," he said. She still didn't seem convinced, so he took a deep breath and admitted, "I lived with someone a few years ago. She didn't want to get married because it would mess up her alimony. She had a little girl. I helped raise her. When we split up, she wouldn't let me see her daughter."

"Wow. How long did you live with them?"

Luke hoped Chloe understood him better now. It

had been difficult for him to tell that story. "Three years."

"That sucks."

"Yeah. So I kind of choke when I see kids."

"You mean when you meet single moms?"

"That too."

"What was your mother thinking?"

"She was thinking I needed to get over myself."

They both laughed, and she rose and walked toward the steps.

"I wouldn't mind going to the game with you tomorrow."

She stopped on her way up the stairs and turned around.

Luke wondered if he'd said that right. Why so hard to figure out the proper words? "What I mean is, I love the Tigers and I'd kill for seats like those. Plotting mothers aside, there's nothing that says we can't be friends."

"We can do that." She had a tiny ghost of a smile on her lips, but he couldn't tell if it reached her eyes because she turned away again and went up the stairs.

Only after he stretched out in bed did he realize the moms had scored a point after all. He was taking a day off, which meant he'd be staying a day longer than he'd planned. And call it whatever, this was a date with Chloe and her sons. He could almost smell the hot dogs and beer.

Chapter Six

Chloe contemplated the contents of her closet. Luke might be cute, but he was not for her. A guy like Luke—who didn't know a good thing when he had it within reach, a guy who let his past hold him back, a guy who thought backward, not forward—a guy like that she could feel empathy for, even be friends with, but as for anything else, no. If he was too afraid of getting hurt to even try, he didn't deserve her. Or her kids. And they were, it went without saying, a package deal.

The move to Seattle would just complicate things more. Sure, people worked out long-distance relationships all the time. Luke didn't seem like the kind of guy to go for that, either. Just a small-town guy content in his little rural world.

So while the boys might be thrilled with Luke joining them at the game, to Chloe, well, she didn't know exactly. And how did one dress for baseball games anyway? Delicious spring-like weather, sunny with a nice breeze. Sneakers and jeans and maybe a three-quarter sleeve T-shirt. Or should she wear short sleeves and bring a jacket? She stared into her open closet door and tried to close down the longing in her heart. For a husband. And a father for her boys. She wondered how many men felt the way Luke did about single moms. Probably lots.

The thought of men, of marriage, even dating, was new. She'd been too busy building her career and raising her sons to date. Now starting anything up seemed pointless since she and the boys would be moving cross-country.

Her protectiveness toward the boys made her wonder why could the men in their lives not see how great the boys were? Although, she had to admit, Luke had been stellar with them yesterday.

"Mommy, when are we leaving?" Josh came into her room and hopped on her bed, his legs kicking out one at a time, because of course impossible to ever be completely still, unless he slept. Both boys were that way. All kids, really. Now that she stayed home with them, she saw their friends more often, and she noted that little boys tended to be in constant motion.

Chloe checked the clock next to her bed.

"In about an hour."

"Do you like Luke?"

Chloe turned away from her wardrobe. The shirt she wore worked just fine. She would kill her mother if she tried in any way to involve the boys in "the plan."

"I do. We're friends like you and Stephen."

"But Luke's a boy and you're a girl. When boys and girls get big, they get married and go on dates."

Chloe laughed. "Usually the other way around."

Intuitive Josh. She predicted this wasn't coming from her mother, who loved the boys enough not to involve them in her crazy schemes if there was any chance on earth they'd be hurt.

"Sometimes. But sometimes it's like you and Emma."

Josh made a face. "I don't play with girls

anymore."

"But you used to. Emma was your best friend. And in a few years, you'll have more girls who are friends."

"Will not!" Josh jumped down off the bed and raced off, the mere thought of a female friend enough to induce a nightmare frenzy.

****

Chloe, Luke, and the boys went to the game in Luke's big truck. He'd washed it that morning, just for the occasion, which touched Chloe. The extended back seat was as roomy as a sedan. From the rear, both boys kept up a steady stream of conversation.

"Luke, do you have one of those riding lawnmowers?"

"I do."

"Where is it?"

"At home. In my box trailer."

"What's a box trailer?"

"Like that." Luke pointed to a trailer without windows hitched to a truck. It did look kind of like a box.

"Do you sleep in there?"

Chloe smiled. Nice for someone else to answer the questions for a change.

"Nope. I sleep in a bed in my house, just like you do."

"Oh."

They'd already been through the favorite player question. Josh liked the only Tiger chosen for the All-Stars so far. Tommy liked Don-O. Josh teased that Tommy hadn't known any of the players' names until Luke said he favored Don. Then all Tommy could say was Don-O, Don-O, Don-O.

Chloe, determined to show her boys that men and women could be just friends, to model behavior for them that would ensure they understood that Luke was not a substitute for their dad, resisted the joy that wanted to break through. Except she enjoyed his company as much as the boys did. She started to add up how long it had been since she'd had sex. So long ago, she couldn't remember. All this free time might be messing with her mind. Thinking about sex had nothing to do with Luke. Although he *was* sexy.

On arrival at the ballpark, the boys wanted to try the batting cages before they even found their seats. They had time before the game started because the kids had been so antsy at home, Luke and Chloe had decided to leave early.

There was plenty to do at the stadium besides watch baseball. While Luke supervised the batting cages, Chloe went to find a bathroom. On her way she kept seeing people with these neon-colored frozen drinks. The skinny glass had to be at least six inches long. Some were blue, others were a combination of colors. Since Luke drove, she'd treat herself to one. She probably should have worn a short sleeved top, because the day was warmer than she'd expected, and an icy-cold girly drink would taste good.

She stood in a short line and noticed the carousel with tigers instead of horses. Cute. They had a lot of things here at the park for kids.

"Mom, can we ride on the baseball?" Josh and Tommy had found her in line.

"What's that?"

"It's a ride."

"Can I have that cup after you're done?"

She could already tell that Tommy would insist on drinking his milk out of the funny shaped glass for the entire summer.

As she sipped her cocktail, yummy but light on the alcohol, they walked around the stadium, checking out the souvenirs, buying a program and a beer for Luke, and foam Tiger paws for the boys.

Tommy and Josh, still too excited to eat or drink anything, begged to go on the baseball Ferris wheel, so the four of them got inside one of the giant baseballs and off they went. They could see the entire Detroit skyline, including the river and into Canada, from their perch.

"That's Windsor," Chloe told Luke. "Drinking age nineteen."

"Sounds like Detroit kids celebrate turning nineteen over there," Luke said.

"Yep."

"Including you?"

"Yep."

"Canada's a whole 'nother country," Josh said.

Eventually, they even watched the game. Both boys wanted to sit next to Luke, and when they claimed their seats, Chloe realized she'd been expecting him to sit next to her. Amid the cacophony of vendors calling "Peanuts! Popcorn! Ice Cream!" fans cheering a run batted in, and the boys peppering Luke with questions, a secret unfolded itself inside Chloe. She could really be serious about Luke. She could see a future with him, all of them as a family. Everything she wanted in the whole wide world was right here in the ball park. The Tigers' victory swept the crowd into a roaring final wave, and soon they were on their way home.

"What a great day," Luke said.

"The best day ever," Tommy agreed.

"I love baseball," Josh enthused.

And I am falling in love with Luke, Chloe thought, before she could stop the progress of emotion rising up in her.

****

Later that night, after the boys had their bath and a snack before bed, after she'd read half a story before Tommy sagged and softly snored on her shoulder, after Josh closed his eyes and curled into his favorite sleeping position, she wandered into the kitchen to fix herself a sandwich and noticed Luke in the garage, trying to catch up, no doubt, on work he'd let slide today. She tried to talk herself out of the crazy idea that she'd fallen in love with him. How could she love him? She hardly knew him!

As soon as she opened the fridge, Luke came in from the garage. She admired how hard he worked.

"Want a sandwich?" she asked.

"Sure." He reached for a beer from the back of the bottom shelf of the fridge while she had the door open.

"Mustard or mayo?"

"Can I have both?"

"Of course. You were great with the boys today. Thanks." She tried to keep her voice as casual as possible when his fingers brushed hers as she handed him the beer he'd been reaching for.

"I love it. They made me feel a like a kid again."

"Especially in that baseball-shaped Ferris wheel."

He rolled his eyes. "You hid your boredom pretty well." If he only knew. She slid bologna onto bread, then slapped the sandwiches together, finally setting them on the table with a flourish worthy of bologna on squishy white bread.

"I don't really get bored when I'm with them. If they're having fun, it's enough for me. It's what I want. It's why I go camping and fishing and, now, to a baseball game."

"You fish?"

She nodded. "I bait the hooks. And then unhook the poor guys and throw them back in."

"You never cook your catch?"

"I draw the line at gutting and skinning." She took a bite of her sandwich. "Spence used to do that, but now, if the boys catch anything, which is not all that often, we throw it back."

"That's no fun."

"It's some fun. Maybe not to you, but they seem to like it okay." Wow. She must be tired. He hadn't called her no fun, just the way she fished. She mentally shook her head. She was an idiot.

They didn't say anything as they finished their sandwiches. Hanging out with Luke, being "friends" was not easy. Especially when his hungry eyes said she was dessert. "I'm gonna hit the sack," she said.

"Don't get lonely," he said.

It took every bit of her courage to keep walking, to not turn around and sit herself down on his lap and kiss him dizzy.

Chapter Seven

Bettina always loved having the boys over, and she felt bad about dropping them off at their mom's in such a hurry again, but Spence had some kind of reaction to his new medication. She wanted to take him to the emergency room, but he refused to go in.

"I just need to sleep," he slurred.

She was so tired, too, that she finally turned the car around and they headed home to bed. In the middle of the afternoon.

The next morning, Bettina's first morning of maternity leave, did not go well. She'd slept maybe four or five fitful hours. Still so tired. But she dressed and combed her hair. One good thing about Spence being out of work, they could have coffee together. Except no caffeine for her for the duration of her pregnancy. Decaf tea, then. Maybe she'd speak to Spence about giving his sponsor a call. He claimed that he could handle a few beers. He had a moderation program. But Bettina had read his prescription bottles, and they all said not to mix with alcohol. Now that she was home, everything would go back to normal.

Spence didn't hear her come into the room. His head full of greasy hair bent over the kitchen table snorting lines of something white with a tiny glass tube.

"What…" She couldn't speak. The words wouldn't come. And the fear she'd managed to hold back while at work hit her like a hurricane. Spence's addiction was loads worse than she'd thought.

Spence's eyes darted up. He pinched his nose and inhaled deeply. His gaze rocketed from the table to her and back again. "Oh hon," he said, "it's not what you think." He got up and poured her a coffee and grabbed a beer from the fridge for himself.

She didn't bother telling him she couldn't have caffeine. Clearly he would not hear her. She glanced at the clock. 9 a.m. Probably even a little earlier. He popped the top on his bottle and drank from it, nothing amiss at all.

He sat, so she did too. Too sad to cry, and she didn't think of herself as a weak woman. As a school principal, she had stood up to male teachers and parents, and a few female bullies as well. But when it came to Spence, her precious love, she had been weak. She felt it now, all energy draining from her. Her heart skidding and skipping. Would it just stop? No. Because she wouldn't let it.

"Just the new meds." Spence slurred the words. "Taking it out of the capsule and snorting it makes it work faster. But this is a pill, so I had to crush it between two spoons to stop the panic attack."

Okay, clearly he was in denial. As had been she.

She couldn't look at him. Instead she inventoried the things on their table. The tube. A few bottles of pills. Two spoons. The cup of untouched coffee Spence had set in front of her.

He didn't put his beer on the table. He held it and took steady sips until he finished it off. His eyes were closed, and he had a stupid grin on his face. She wanted to slap it off.

Chloe moving the boys to Seattle. Spence had not taken that well. Things had gotten worse, not better, when he saw a doctor to deal with his depression over the boys moving.

Bettina's sadness went deep under the skin. Soon they'd have their own child. They had planned it: he the stay-at-home dad, taking care of the baby and working on polishing his Realtor skills as the economy slowly began to rebound.

The baby kicked. As if telling Bettina to get in gear. Handle this problem. Spence tried to reach the fridge without getting out of his chair and fell to the floor. He laughed. Tempting to blame Spence's relapse on Chloe, but the only person to blame was the guy doing the drugging. He did not have to say yes to Chloe. Bettina still wasn't sure why he had. He hadn't consulted her or talked it over with her. One day, it just happened. Spence's soft snores lifted to her ears. At least he wasn't dead.

She got out of her chair, which in her condition took a minute or two. Then she went into Spence's "office" where he "worked." He hadn't bothered to hide his stash. She found it in the first drawer she opened.

He claimed to have a prescription for medical marijuana, but the pint jar came from her summer strawberry jam making. Somehow, she didn't think she'd be making any jam this summer. She kept to her inventory. Two bags of loose pills, many pills, maybe fifty in each bag, with no prescription label attached. Six bottles, some for sleep, some for anxiety, one for ADHD. Also two more prescriptions, from two different doctors, filled at two different drugstores, for pain. What pain? She continued to search and came up with a roach clip topped with a dice for ease of handling, a pipe he liked to smoke his weed in, and rolling papers.

She knew about some of these drugs. She knew about one doctor. There were drugs he said had made him sick so he had to switch to another. However, the pill bottles told a different story. He still filled both prescriptions. For the first time, she knew why Chloe had left Spence. He'd been to rehab, gotten clean, and Chloe had left him anyway. It hadn't made sense to Bettina until now. Now she understood that Spence might have had more than one rehab and relapse experience. She went back down to check on him. Still out cold. Now what?

The prescriptions had been from four different doctors and five different drug stores. They were all legal, as far as she knew. Wasn't it illegal to go to lots of doctors to obtain lots of drugs? Why hadn't she educated herself beyond the usual school in-service programs for faculty and staff held once every few years? She'd gone to these in-services. About her job, she listened. Just had not connected any of it to her personal life.

No one had mentioned crushing pills with spoons. Spoons were for cooking heroin. Glass pipes were for smoking crack. She checked the back of the spoons. No dark smudging. Okay. Right. He'd probably told her the truth about crushing the tablets with two spoons. Capsules made it that much easier. Should she call these doctors? And if she did, would Spence go to jail? Would her baby be born with daddy in prison?

Her anger slipped out from where she usually kept it tucked inside. She went back downstairs to the kitchen and kicked Spence's bare foot. She told herself she was trying to rouse him. He snored louder, didn't move. She filled her largest soup pot with cold water, and almost threw it on him, but then reconsidered. She'd be the one cleaning it up. She reached for her phone and pressed speed dial.

"Oh hon, I'm so sorry," Chloe said after Bettina had told her the entire story.

"Thank you, but what should I do?"

Chloe didn't say anything, but Bettina could hear her breathing on the line. "Is that an unfair question? Maybe, can I ask, what did you do?"

"I never turned him in. He went willingly."

"How many times?"

"Just twice. Once before Josh was born. And then right before I left him. I said if he went to rehab I'd stay, but I lied."

"So what set him off this time? Our baby? Your move?"

"Don't." Chloe kept her voice low. "It's not us; it's him. Nothing you can do or say or be will stop him if he chooses to get high, go off program. Is he attending meetings?"

"I'm not sure." Bettina doubted he'd gone to the moderation group any time lately. Who goes on a modification plan and has a beer first thing in the morning? "He's doing this moderation plan he found online. Where they have this elaborate set up: no drinking two days in a row, never more than two drinks per day, never drink alone."

"Was he abiding by the plan?" Disbelief clear in Chloe's tone.

"I'm not sure. I don't think so. I just started

maternity leave today!"

"Oh, Bettina. I'm really sorry. I put faith in rehab to take this time. I thought maybe you were the one who could turn him around."

"But you just said. It's not me. It's not you. It's not anything we do or don't do. He decides to drink. And drug."

They were silent a beat.

"He still out?"

Bettina kicked his foot, a little harder this time. He rolled over. Her foot so close to his face. She had to work hard to hold herself back from bashing his nose in with it. "Yeah."

"Do you have his sponsor's phone number?"

"No. They no longer have a relationship. Because Spence drinks."

"Right."

"Do you know if it's illegal to drug shop? Because he has all those doctors?"

"No. I really don't. Google it."

"Thanks. I'll keep you in the loop."

Bettina thought about calling 9-1-1. What would she say? Something like "My husband is unconscious."

And they'd ask "Is he breathing?"

Then she'd have to admit he was snoring. Can someone who has overdosed snore?

When Bettina searched online for "medication from different doctors" she found an article about "pill shopping" and it fit close enough to Spence's case. The person buying the pills got charged with a misdemeanor. Surely, if she turned him in, a judge would have mercy on a man with a wife about to give birth to their first child? But maybe not. She was so scared, she didn't know what to do. She had nobody to ask without jeopardizing her husband's freedom.

The next question Bettina asked herself, sitting with her fingers over the keyboard, is would six weeks be long enough? The answer was no. Spence had a bad relapse problem. So he'd likely miss the baby's first weeks at home, too. Then she thought about leaving a six-week-old baby with an addict. Even an addict in recovery.

Her slippery slope thinking stopped. She'd tell him to get clean or they were over. She'd find a nanny for the baby. She loved Spence, but she loved her baby more.

****

After Sunday's baseball game, Luke kept busy in the backyard. They'd gone back a step. But it wasn't. Not really. They'd shared a day, not a date. And Luke had work to do. The boys were busy with school. Her mother made frequent trips to Blue Lake, slowly emptying her home in Sterling Pines of a lifetime's worth of treasures. Everyone around her being all active and engaged while Chloe dangled, her time loose. When had she last been so free of responsibility? Maybe when Josh was born.

Chloe jogged. She practiced yoga. She went online to search for houses in Seattle. Nothing appealed to her. Kristy had set Chloe and the boys up in a corporate condo for as long as she needed it. She had no pressing engagements and nothing to do with her time but paint her toenails bright red.

As she sat on a kitchen chair, hunched around her toes with a tiny brush full of red polish ready to go, Luke came into the house, startling her into painting her entire baby toe. She let out a little yelp of frustration.

"You okay?" he asked.

She tightened the brush into the bottle of polish and got her feet under the table where he couldn't see them.

"Yeah, you just startled me."

"Sorry." He stood on the landing, so she wasn't sure if he meant to head downstairs or up, but his eyes were trained under the table, assessing her botched pedicure. "Red, huh?"

Yep. He'd noticed.

"I need a little color in my life."

He came into the kitchen, poured a tall glass of water, and sat down across the table from her.

"Are you a, what do they call it, stay-at-home mom?"

She smiled. Yes, for the moment. And she really enjoyed it. Most of the time.

"I start my new job after Mom moves to Blue Lake." Should she say it was in Seattle? No. Why would it matter to him? "The boys and I are taking our usual vacation up there after school lets out."

"Will you stay with your mom?"

"Usually we do. But it's crowded, and I want to try that new place with the cottages."

"Blue Heaven. I went to high school with the owner. You should book it soon. Those cottages fill up quick."

"I've been meaning to do that," she said.

"I can check for you." He hit the keys on his cell.

He seemed more interested in her vacation than asking where or what her job involved. Fine with her. But why? Was she afraid if she told him about Seattle, he'd lose all interest in her? It wasn't like he'd really shown all that much anyway. Until now. Now he wanted to make sure she had a place to stay when she came to his town.

"All full," he said, showing her the picture on his phone of the cottage schedule for Blue Heaven.

"Darn. I guess we'll be cooped up with Mom again. I really wanted to be on the water."

"I can call my buddy. His wife used to live in the main house until they got married. Now she rents it out to select guests."

"Maybe I'm not so select."

"Yeah, you are. I know Daniel and Eva, and my mom works there. Want me to give them a call? They don't advertise the house, so the only way to get in is to call and ask."

"Okay," she said. "Thanks." She checked her phone calendar and gave him the dates.

He called right then and got it all set up. Didn't even ask for a credit card.

"Are you hungry?" she asked when he replaced the phone into his pocket. She could make him a thank-you lunch.

"I could eat," he said. Their eyes locked, and the air charged with energy that felt like something else. Something that didn't appear in any of the food groups.

She got up and opened the fridge. She found turkey and cheese and then bent over to check the veggie bin. She turned to ask if he liked lettuce and tomato on his sandwich and caught him staring at her butt. She forgot what she meant to ask him and shut the fridge without pulling anything out.

"What do you like?" she asked, leaning against the fridge.

He got up to refill his glass of water. He didn't answer for a minute, just stood at the sink, his back to her, drinking his water. Then he turned around and let her see the hunger in his eyes. He walked the four paces it took to reach her and pulled her into his arms for a long, delicious kiss.

She'd been kissed a lot in her life, but never ever like this. His mouth on hers took her to another place, fully in her body but unaware of the kitchen and the fact that her mother could walk in, back from the grocery store, at any moment. Nothing else but Luke existed for the length of his kiss. Every time he started to move away, she pulled him back, and they kissed some more. She kissed him for every day before that when she hadn't been able to. She kissed him and asked him with her kiss to care about her the way she cared about him.

The slam of her mother's car door in the driveway stopped the kiss. They pulled slowly away from each other, but he kept his eyes glued to hers. "I want you," he said.

"I want you, too." And then she went out and helped her mother bring the groceries into the house.

She counted down the days until Luke would finish his projects and leave. Three. Two. One. And in those three days, there had been no vibe of desire. Zero kissing.

****

The day before Luke left, Josh and Tommy went for a weekend with their dad. Bettina, one hand on her small of her back, watered flowers in the front yard. Chloe didn't see Spence, so she got out and walked over to Bettina, the boys already racing into the house.

They were excited, as usual, to spend time with Spence, who they adored despite his shortcomings as a father. They'd said distracted good-byes to Luke, who kept his own good-bye equally short, although he stopped rolling sod long enough to watch them pull out of the driveway.

"You know he's going home after tomorrow," Chloe said to the boys as she turned the corner to Spence's house.

"Yeah, but Grandma's moving to Luke's town, so we'll see him all the time."

Her Seattle secret burned in her throat, even as she asked Bettina, the boys out of earshot, "How's Spence?"

Bettina turned the water faucet off and put both arms behind her back, rubbing and stretching.

"He's upset about the boys."

"I'm sure he is, but what else is going on?"

Bettina bent her head. Groaned as she reached to pull out a dandelion.

"He's promised to shape up. We had a huge fight, well, a discussion. He saw his doctor and is on a new medication. The others just weren't cutting it for him."

Bettina's eyes welled. "He admitted he'd been pill shopping. His meds just stopped working, and he was over-medicating. So now there's a fresh cocktail."

"Does the doctor know that Spence drinks along with all the other drugs?" Chloe hated the confrontational tone of her words, so she put her hand on Bettina's arm. "I'm worried about you."

A few tears dropped down Bettina's cheeks. She dashed them away. "Everything will be fine when the baby gets here. His new meds will kick in, and we'll be good."

Chloe nodded. For Bettina's sake, she hoped it was true.

"I mean—" Bettina blushed. "He'll miss the boys, of course."

"I know. And they'll still see each other. I promise."

"Thank you." Bettina rested her head on Chloe's shoulder.

"You're welcome." Chloe pulled her into a hug. "I love you, I love how you take care of my boys. Our boys."

They both left unsaid the raw fact that Spence was just another one of the boys for Bettina to worry about.

Chapter Eight

By the time Chloe got home, Luke had finished the sod and had started on the shrubs. They said quick hellos as he ambled back down the driveway toward his work and she returned to the house.

Her mother chopped veggies at the counter in the kitchen, preparing a big salad. Their tradition. The boys were not fans of salad, so when they went away for the weekend, that's what Ursula and Chloe ate for dinner. Except after the ball game, Josh had eaten salad. Because Luke did. Chloe didn't think she should tell her mom that.

"I've been meaning to tell you…" Ursula said. Chloe pulled out a couple of plates and forks and sat down at the table to wait for her mom to join her. "The couple who were interested in the house before? The ones who said they'd reconsider if I got the place up to code? They made an offer."

"Oh, Mom, that's great."

"They drove by and saw all the work being done and called the Realtor. They were afraid someone else would snap this place up."

"I'm really happy for you, Mom."

"It doesn't bother you that I've sold your childhood home?"

"No. It's time. We all need to move on with our lives." Chloe risked choking up but said what was on her mind anyway. "I am so grateful you took us in when I left Spence. I would not be where I am today without your help."

"What, unemployed and single?"

"I've accepted a great offer for a dream job. It's a huge step up from what I did at Rob's firm." Chloe forked a jumbo bite of salad and stuffed it in her mouth so she wouldn't be able to say anything else.

"And do the boys know about this job?" Her mom put her fork down even though she'd just speared it with greens.

Chloe, chewing away, didn't answer. Instead, she shook her head.

"Does Luke?"

Chloe swallowed, and a piece of carrot went down the wrong pipe. She coughed and drank water. "What does he have to do with anything?" But she knew more than her mother did about how much he had to do with everything.

"Because I can't help but think it's my fault. I move two hours north, and you go clear across the country."

Chloe kept sipping her water, her eyes tearing. She coughed a few times to pretend the food choked, but she knew darn well where her pain came from now.

She wanted Luke. She didn't just want to have sex with him. She wanted a life with him. And she was afraid he wouldn't want her enough to commit to a long-distance relationship. Crazy to think something like that could work for the long term, but maybe if they got to know each other slowly, if they kept in touch via Skype, phone calls, texts, frequent visits…it didn't seem impossible. It couldn't be impossible.

Her mother got up from the table and rinsed her plate. Chloe did the same, even though it remained half full of healthy green stuff.

"Mom. Stop a minute." Her mother was already busy going through cabinets. She threw a set of measuring cups into a cardboard box. Cardboard boxes were in every room.

"I can pack and talk at the same time." Her mother's voice had an edge to it.

God, she hated this. Did every single parent have to make such tough choices? She should have known she'd have to pay eventually. It had been way too easy, moving in with Mom, working for Rob, seeing the boys every night, and telling herself that she had to earn a living for all of them. And that was still true.

"Mom, I am not doing this to hurt you. I am doing it so that my children can go to college. So that they will have a good life. I thank you for all you did for us. I love you, you know that."

Her mother nodded, contemplating pot-holders.

"You were right to sell this place. We were all stuck here. We've been stuck since Dad died. It's time to move on."

Her mom began to cry; Chloe did, too.

"I'll be taking my furniture, but you're welcome to keep your old bedroom set."

If anything proved to Chloe that she needed to grab this Seattle opportunity, that did. She still slept on the twin bed she'd had since she graduated from a crib. She should probably get a new bed. And her own furniture. Way past time. Why did it feel so scary? Was she imagining her feelings for Luke as a way out of moving so far away?

"I'm sorry, honey. I feel like I started something here, and it turned into another thing when I had my head turned."

"It's just life. There wouldn't ever be a perfect time for me to get out on my own."

Her mom nodded and got up from the table again. She covered the serving bowl of salad with plastic wrap and put it in the fridge for Luke.

"No sense calling him in to eat. He won't stop until he waters those plants."

"He can't wait to get home." Chloe got up from the table, too. "He did a great job," she said. And then, "Please don't tell him about Seattle."

Her mother looked up from a pile of stained tea towels, alert at Chloe's unexpected request. She thought for a minute and then put the tea towels in the box.

"He has a good business there, you know," her mother said. "People depend on him. I was lucky to get him when I did. But he's got jobs stacked up, just waiting. That's why he's working so hard. Wanda says this time of year he's always really busy."

Chloe knew she'd fanned her mom's hopes by mentioning Luke. "Please, Mom."

"I won't tell him a thing," her mother said.

"You won't tell Wanda?"

"No. Not until you're gone. Then it won't matter anyway."

"That's fine. Say whatever you want after I leave. I just want to relax with the boys for a week without having all the people in your new town judging me."

Her mom didn't reply to that. Instead she went downstairs for another packing box.

****

The next morning, Chloe opened the fridge to find cream for her coffee. She noticed the salad her mom had set aside for Luke still sealed in plastic wrap. When she saw Luke's packed duffel bag at the back door, she headed for the sugar bowl and gave herself an extra teaspoon.

The deserted yard glowed with loving care.

With coffee in hand, Chloe walked into the living room. From the picture window, she saw that Luke had already loaded his truck and stood talking to her mother. She wondered, if she hadn't come out of the bedroom, would he have even said good-bye? How could he stick by his stupid rule after that kiss? How dare he make her fall in love with him and then turn off?

Luke gazed toward the house and saw her standing at the window. He walked around the back. The kitchen door opened, and she went back in to meet him. He already had his duffel bag in hand.

"I guess this is good-bye for now," he said.

"I'll see you soon."

"Chloe, I—"

"What?"

"I do want you. I want to date you. I want to hang out with the boys and watch baseball and go fishing. But you'll be here and I'll be there—" He dropped his duffel. "Hell, even when we're in the same house, we can't get any time together."

"If by that you mean sex, well, I can't disrespect my mother or confuse my kids by carrying on a secret affair."

"Of course not. I didn't mean to imply that."

A crushing sadness made it hard for her to answer.

Even with the little time he had left after working all day and half into the night, he could have more openly displayed his feelings toward her in front of her family. Touched her hand when she poured him coffee. Kissed her on the cheek even. Said little things to the boys to start to get them adjusted to Luke being in their lives. But he hadn't. And that could only mean one thing. He didn't have a serious interest in her. Okay, that's why her chest hurt. He'd reached inside her and ripped her heart in two.

But he was the smart one, smarter than he knew, and she was numb. Numb and dumb.

They were both quiet for a minute, and then he picked up his duffel again, said good-bye again, and walked out the door.

****

Spence rallied. He had his routine down and would not let his selfish hurt feelings interfere with this last weekend with his boys. So it hurt to see his kids leave? Nobody's fault but his own. He deserved it.

Josh and Tommy kept talking about some dude who lived with them. "Luke went to the ball game with us, Dad. He's never even been to Detroit before."

"Sounds like a hick."

They were eating on the sofa, something Bettina didn't allow, but she was napping and Spence didn't like her rules anyway. This was his house. He had made them big sandwiches with pickles and chips and peanut butter and jelly. He layered the chips and pickles on each side. The boys loved them.

"What's a hick?"

"Oh, just someone who's never been to the big city."

"Mom likes him. Maybe they'll get married like you and Bettina."

"Doubtful," Spence said, thinking about opening a beer for about the tenth time in the last five minutes. He hoisted himself up. "Cookies?"

"Yes!" Two replies in one. He would miss these little pissers. They were so damn cute. Tommy had lost his front tooth, and his smile made Spence's heart pang.

He grabbed an unopened bag of cookies from the pantry and took a quick shot of whiskey before snagging a beer. He remembered the days back when he had been the tooth fairy.

He re-entered the living room, his body tilting as he threw the cookie bag in the air. The boys scrambled to catch it, but it landed behind the sofa. Spence laughed and sipped his beer while Tommy leaned over the sofa for the cookies. His arm didn't reach. Spence downed the beer and crushed the can. He went over to the sofa and picked Tommy up by the legs, dangling him over the cookies.

Tommy giggled and grabbed the cookies. Spence scooped him into his arms and set him down carefully. He messed with Josh's hair because he knew Josh wouldn't let anybody but his dad do that. Not even a hick named Luke.

Bettina came downstairs at dinner time, but none of them were hungry. They'd just watched a Sponge Bob marathon. That show was deep, Spence thought, if you really read between the lines. He saw the floor where his crushed beer can lay. Oh boy. Trouble if she sees that. He'd never started drinking with the kids still around.

He jumped up and ran over to Bettina. He hugged

her and kissed her. "Good morning, sleeping beauty."

"She's not sleeping, Dad!" Josh laughed.

"She's a beauty, though," Spence said. Bettina smiled. It looked forced. Despite his efforts, she'd seen the beer can. Or tasted whisky on his tongue, or both.

"Want to play cards?" Josh asked.

"Time to start dinner. Tacos!" Bettina said.

"I'm too full for dinner," Tommy said, his eyes sliding to the empty cookie bag on the coffee table.

"Me too," Josh said.

"Okay, we'll play some cards, and maybe you'll be hungry later," Bettina said.

"Give me a sec, guys," Spence said. "Gotta break the seal." The boys laughed hard whenever he said that. Bettina just shook her head.

He went up and took a pill. The one for anxiety. His wife was about to yell at him, but she'd yell softly, in their room, after the boys were in bed. He didn't want to ruin the whole day by being anxious about his nighttime scolding.

He kept a supply of liquor in his office now, so he drank down the pill with whisky straight from the bottle. Then he went to play cards with his family.

Poor Spence, he thought, after the tenth card game. The boys were helping Bettina assemble the taco fixings as he sat in front of the evening news, not caring about Syria or space junk. Better not to see them at all than see them leave over and over again. What an ass he'd been. A self-centered whiny ass. He was the parent. He needed to be strong for his boys. Now with the aid of a nice drug cocktail and a whisky kick, he felt okay most days.

The tacos were good, and the boys went to bed

right on time. Now he could get down to it.

Drinking was the best thing. His sponsor didn't think so, had ended their relationship, and told Spence to get back in touch when he wanted to get sober. His moderation group had such crazy, arbitrary rules. Only drink every other day. One drink per hour. No more than two drinks. No, he'd done with them. Whisky and music, flat out rock, none of that twangy folk stuff, no rhymers either. He drank, he soared, he smoked, he slept.

He woke on the sofa when he heard Tommy asking Josh why dad only had one ear bud in. He pulled it out.

"Morning, boys!" His head might split in two. He slanted his eyes toward the coffee table. Thank God. Clean. They hadn't seen the remains of his party for one. Good old Bettina. She understood. She'd cleaned up his mess.

This was the first time he'd done his thing with them here in the house. He'd always reserved it for Sunday, just after they left. It dulled the pain of saying good-bye again. And he'd tried to abstain. Friday night went okay. They'd gone out to one of those restaurants that catered to kids. Anxiety always called for an extra pill to mellow him out. Also, it made him fall asleep almost as soon as they got home.

He thought he could make it through one more day. But something wicked got hold of him. This was the last time he'd see them for a very long time. They were leaving Michigan for good, and there wasn't a thing he could do about it.

"Daddy, you stink!" Tommy giggled.

Spence tried to smile at his younger son, but his neck couldn't hold up his head.

"He hasn't showered yet," Josh explained. Spence saw from Josh's expression that he knew more than Tommy about what had actually happened. "Bettina's making pancakes, Dad. Better hurry and get cleaned up."

Spence tried to stand and immediately felt dizzy, like he might be sick—and then—too late. Last night's tacos were splashed down his shirt, on the sofa, even the rug.

"Bettina," Tommy yelled, alarmed. "Dad's sick."

His wife came out to the living room, took one look at the situation, went back into the kitchen, and came back with a wet cloth. She threw it at his face, and he did a quick mop up as the boys stood rooted in fascinated confusion. Josh's nose wrinkled again. The smell of burnt pancakes mingled with his vomit.

"Daddy couldn't get up! We should take him to the hospital," Tommy said.

"No," Spence managed to rasp, carefully rising from the sofa. "It's just something I ate is all."

"There was an empty whiskey bottle on the table when we got up," Josh said.

Bettina called the boys to come eat their pancakes while they were hot.

So the boys had seen his mess. Beer cans, his pipe, and that damn whiskey. He started to bend down to use the towel on the rug, but lost heart and left it there. He managed to get up the stairs and into the shower, leaving his soiled shirt where he dropped it.

Then, as he struggled to turn the hot water on, Tommy was at the door. "It's okay, Daddy. I can help. Maybe you should have a bath instead of a shower?"

Spence, naked, sat on the toilet lid and let his little

boy draw him a bath. He started to cry. A grown man crying in front of his little son.

Tommy took Spence's face into his tiny hands. "It's okay, Daddy. We saved you some pancakes."

"Jesus fuck," Spence said, tears streaming and snot forming under his nose. Still drunk. Had to be. He never swore around his boys.

Tommy's eyes popped wide. He slammed his hands over his mouth and ran out of the room.

Spence got his shaking body into the tub. He let himself sink under, washing away the stink. He managed a half-assed hair and body wash and let the water drain out. He couldn't find it in him to get out of that empty tub. He hugged his knees, put his head down, and cried.

Bettina saw him in all his wretchedness. She used to be kinder when he had these days, but these days had grown to every day, and her tolerance and pity were all used up.

"Get out," she said.

At first he thought she meant get out of the house. But she held a towel open, and he gingerly rose from the tub, sniffing back his sobs. She didn't wrap the towel around him. She shoved it at his belly, and he had to act fast and grab it before it fell. Without another word, she walked out the door. Then she turned around and came back in the room. He still dripped, still held the towel to himself. "You're disgusting. Your last day with the boys, and you'll be no use to them." She grabbed the soiled clothing off the floor.

****

"Bettina, what's wrong with Daddy?" Tommy wanted to know.

"Is he mad at us because we're moving?" Josh had that look of concentration he got when he thought too hard.

This had to be hard for her, too. She loved these boys as if they were her own. They'd been happy and excited when she got pregnant, and she'd tried her best to shield them from the worst of Spence's excessive addiction. She finally admitted it to herself. He was an addict. Not a former alcoholic, not a reformed druggie, not a doper in recovery, but the opposite of sober, every damn light lit up like Christmas.

"No, I think he has the flu."

"Well, then, why did he use the bad swear? First he said Jesus, and I thought he was praying but then he said the F word."

"Is Dad going to hell?" Josh asked. Bettina wondered if in her fury she had told Spence to go to hell.

"No, honey," she said. "Why did you think that?"

"Because that's a very bad swear."

Okay, maybe she'd hadn't blown up, at least with words that could be misunderstood by small children. Still, it was awful. She and Spence rarely argued, and never in front of the children. That awful word "enabling" labeled the problem neatly. She'd been afraid to confront him about his relapse. She pretended it wasn't so bad. At first it wasn't, but soon he became as out of control as she'd ever seen him.

"He cried so he knew he shouldn't have said it," Tommy reasoned.

Spence still hadn't come down after a half hour, and Bettina admitted to herself that he was in his dope den, smoking his pipe. Smoking calmed him, so maybe the day could be salvaged after all. They could lie low, watch a video, play cards.

When she got up this morning, the boys had been in the family room with a passed-out Spence. They took turns pretending to drink from the bottle of whiskey, passing it back and forth, and laughing quietly. Bettina didn't worry that they'd actually drank any of it. Spence had never met a whiskey bottle he couldn't empty. She'd smiled at the boys and asked them to help clean up Dad's mess. It broke her heart to say that. She scooped up the pipe, and they each took a couple of beer cans. Josh kept the whiskey bottle and rinsed it out at the sink before placing it carefully in the recycle bin.

Chapter Nine

Chloe, bereft, dangled in the empty space around her. Less than a week after Luke left, her mother too had gone, off to start a new life in Blue Lake. The life Chloe knew seemed irretrievably lost. Like a distant cheerleader, Kristy kept in touch, but whenever Chloe thought about changing her life so drastically, her mood fell flat while her anxiety climbed. Was she doing the right thing? When should she tell the boys?

Packing their own boxes, Josh brought up the subject. "This is a lot of stuff for vacation, Mom."

"While we're on vacation, the new people will move in, and we'll go somewhere else."

"Where? Are we going to live with Grandma again?" Tommy wanted to know.

"No, dummy. Grandma's new house is too small."

"Don't call me dummy! Mommy, he called me dummy!"

"Josh, Tommy's right. Don't call him names. Tommy, Josh is right, we're not living with Grandma anymore. Well, maybe sometime, when we move to a new place, we'll have lots of bedrooms, and Grandma can come to stay with us. Would you like that?"

Tommy nodded his head, but Josh still had questions.

"Where will we live? Will I still go to my same school?"

91

"No, sweetie. You'll both go to a new school. In Seattle."

"Where's Seattle?"

"It's in another state. Where Mommy has a new job."

"But I don't want to leave my friends. Stephen is my best friend. I don't want to leave him. Or my school. Or my other friends. Emma!"

"Honey, I'm sorry. But you'll make new friends." Chloe knew this would be difficult, but at least nobody cried.

They continued to pack up the boys' room. Three piles: one to keep, one to donate, one to throw away. Tommy didn't want to throw away anything, even a puzzle missing half its pieces. Josh said he didn't care what they brought; it wouldn't matter if they couldn't bring Stephen.

"What about Daddy?" Josh said it like an accusation.

"Daddy's not moving, but you will still see him every summer and at Christmas."

"What about weekends?"

"We have to wait and see."

Tommy started to cry. Then Josh. Chloe knew she was supposed to be the strong adult, but as she gathered her precious boys into her arms, she cried, too.

****

Luke pushed the paperwork for his quarterly taxes away and picked up his ringing phone. Another new customer. The population in Blue Lake continued to age, and as they aged, they needed more help in their yards, which was good for business, but also sad.

He turned off his coffeepot and grabbed his keys

from the hook next to the door. He hadn't thought about Chloe once yet today. Well, unless you counted thinking about not thinking about her. And it was early yet.

He knew his schedule by heart, but double checked it again because at least that way he wouldn't be thinking about Chloe. Grrrr. Maybe it was time to break his rule. Maybe when she came up with her boys for vacation, he should ask her out. He bet she cut a fine-ass figure in a bathing suit.

After work that day, like on every other Friday since the day he turned twenty-one, Luke met his buddies at Fast Eddie's for a few beers. Eddie kept most of his huge barn of a place, with stage and dance floor areas, partitioned off most of the winter. But during tourist season, every seat filled. When Chloe walked in with Eva, the owner of Blue Heaven, talking and laughing like old friends, she didn't even notice him in the throngs of people as some clown offered his seat at the bar. She and Eva sat, and Eddie himself gave them each a glass of wine.

Where were the boys? Where were Josh and Tommy? Funny how that was his first thought. It wasn't like Chloe to leave them alone on their first night of vacation. He noticed how Chloe's long legs were already tanned, and how she dressed in raggedly cut-off jeans and a red tank top. She looked good. Fit and healthy and happy. She lifted the wine to her lips and laughed at something Eva said before she drank.

Eddie set down several take-out bags on the counter, and both opened their wallets at the same time.

"Hot summer chick with Eva Bryman," one of his buddies remarked. Finn. He was always hitting on the summer chicks.

"She's got two kids," Luke said. It just sort of slipped out.

"You know her?"

"Yeah. That's the job I took in May downstate."

"So you hit that while you were there?"

"Shut up, Finn. She lives with her kids."

"Sorry."

Eva and Chloe gathered the bags of food. Luke knew they'd take it back to Blue Heaven. Decision time. Now or never. Break his number one rule or let her go.

"You don't mind if I go by the bonfire later and strike up a conversation with her? What's her name anyway?"

"Chloe. And no. Why should I mind?" But he did. His plan to woo Chloe had gotten no further than somehow easing into a more personal relationship. Somehow. And even then, he wasn't sure. He'd made his rule for a reason, and it had saved him from certain trouble a few times in the past.

But later, after the sun went down and the bonfire at Blue Heaven blazed, Luke drove slowly by the resort. Finn's car stood out. Eva and Daniel didn't mind the locals mingling with their guests, and Daniel and Finn were friends.

Daniel and Eva were good people. Rich people, but not stuck up. He wasn't rich, but he didn't do so bad. He could support a family. He pulled into the state park lot next to Blue Heaven and got out of his car. He leaned against his car hood and listened to the bonfire sounds. He thought he heard Tommy ask for another s'more. Then, when Chloe laughed and said yes, he was sure. He loved her laugh.

Then, when he thought he saw Finn next to Chloe through the trees, he moved closer to Eva and Daniel's property line. There were no fences, just a dense stand of trees, and he went halfway into them before he hesitated.

He peered through the darkness, through the bonfire flames, at Chloe. Finn wasn't sitting next to her at all. She had Tommy on one side of her and Josh on the other. The boys held sticks with marshmallow tips. Chloe put chocolate squares into graham crackers. Finn was on the other side of the fire, his back to Luke. He'd changed his shirt from earlier, but Luke knew his straight blond hair. Finn wore it long, like a surfer dude, even though Lake Huron had no surf. The ladies liked it, Finn always claimed, when the guys razzed him about his hippie hair.

Luke's eyes moved back to Chloe's face, so dreamy in the firelight. He wondered how she was doing. What was happening with the new job, her housing situation? She must live somewhere else by now. Somewhere new. Probably not here in Blue Lake. His mother hadn't said a word, and neither had Ursula, who had hired him to cut her lawn.

His heart rose in his chest with a thought. Maybe she didn't have a new house yet. She could move here. Maybe she'd fall in love with Blue Lake the way her mother had. Maybe she'd fall in love with him. It was hard to see her, even at a distance, without wanting to touch her.

He'd missed her and the boys more than he thought he would. What good was a rule that didn't help when you needed it? If she came back here for good, he'd always have her in front of him. If he didn't act soon, Finn or another of his friends would get her first. She'd marry one of them maybe. He couldn't let that happen. He had to make his move and make it quick.

"Mom, did you hear something?" Josh. Always alert. Nothing passed by that kid.

"No, honey. Where?"

"There." Josh pointed to right where he stood, camouflaged by foliage and the night.

Chloe peered into the trees through the darkness, but didn't see anything except shadows and pines. Everywhere she'd looked today, she had hoped to see Luke. But she hadn't seen him, and it was unlikely he'd be lurking in the trees.

"Just a critter," Daniel, Eva's husband, said.

Josh accepted that answer. Chloe sighed. He'd been different, sad, since school had ended and he'd realized they were leaving Sterling Pines. When her boy turned his carefully toasted marshmallow toward her, Chloe angled the chocolate filled graham cracker under and above the perfectly toasted marshmallow and pressed down, forming the s'more. When she handed it to Josh, she turned to Tommy to help make his treat. Tommy's marshmallow was burned on all sides, although he claimed he liked 'em like that.

Chloe contemplated the full moon and missed Luke so much she wouldn't have been surprised to see it break. Surely they'd run into each other here. Blue Lake was a small town. His mother worked at Blue Heaven. She'd met Wanda that afternoon. She'd explained the way Blue Heaven worked. The big house had private quarters, but also an office and a second story where the cottagers could gather from eight in the morning until midnight. Wanda would wait until Chloe unlocked the private quarters to come change the sheets and refresh the towels.

"Just give me the high sign, and I'll take care of y'all." Her smile had reminded Chloe of Luke. But neither one of them had mentioned him.

Eva and Chloe were the last two at the fire, long after the boys, Eva's husband Daniel, and the other guests had gone to bed. They talked and talked. About their lives, their loves, their careers, their disasters. Eva was from downstate, just like Chloe, but that's about all their lives had in common. Eva married to a wonderful man, and Chloe divorced a drug-addicted alcoholic.

"He wasn't always that way," Chloe said. Nobody in their right mind marries a man with as many issues as Spence.

"What happened?" Eva poked the fire with a stick and sparks flew into the sky. She threw another log on, signaling that she wanted details.

"He lost his job in '07."

"That's when everything started to go to hell."

"Yes. So I went to work. I happened into a good job using skills I never dreamed I'd need."

"Sounds kind of like what happened to me when Daniel and I restored this place."

"Yeah, I'm good at managing people, matching contract workers with businesses. And these days nearly everyone in Michigan is a contract worker. I found my niche. And it saved our home."

"But killed your marriage."

"Something like that. It started slow. The drinking. Smoking a little weed here and there. And it just continued to get worse. To the point that I forced him into rehab. He came out a changed man. For a minute."

Chloe was quiet for a while, remembering what Bettina had said last time they'd seen each other. "So back he went into rehab, and when he got out, I had already moved to my mom's with the kids. I told him to stay straight for a year, and I'd consider working on our marriage. He lasted about two minutes that time."

"Some men."

"He's a good man, but his addictions got the best of him. I don't know. It seems so stupid and trite. Only a failure loses his job and his wife has to support the family, so he drowns his sorrows, smokes them away, pops another pill..."

"Oh wow, so he's still a mess? How does he survive?"

"I paid the house off and gave it to him." Chloe didn't include the part about how she bribed him into letting the boys go to Seattle. She felt a twinge about that. Bettina had hinted that her move had been why Spence's addictions escalated. "And he married the principal of the boys' school."

"What?"

"Yeah, he got her while clean. She fell for the single dad thing. Now she's expecting a baby, and he's just falling deeper into addiction. I hate it. I hate that my kids have to see it."

"Sometimes, life sucks."

"Yes, it does. But not tonight."

Chapter Ten

Bettina enrolled in a summer class, hoping for a promotion. If Spence didn't clean up his act, she would have to leave him. Just like his last wife had. She saw Chloe's point of view so clearly now. She pulled in the driveway, wondering what she'd encounter when she opened the front door.

Same old, same old. Spence passed out on the sofa, a burn hole in the carpet where he'd dropped a lit roach, still on the clip. He could have destroyed their home. He could have died in a fire. God, she couldn't go on this way.

Spence opened one eye. "Whoa. Hi, hon. Fell asleep."

"Yeah, guess you did."

"What time is it?"

"After six."

"Oh shit. I'm sorry. I meant to make you dinner."

"That's fine. I have a protein shake, and there's leftover pizza." She flatlined, defeated. This was supposed to be the happiest time of her life, but she was truly miserable. She sat on the edge of the sofa and kicked off her shoes. Before she realized it, she wiped away tears.

"Aw, now don't start that crying shit."

That just made her cry harder.

Spence got up and went to the fridge for a beer.

She heard the tab pop, then heard him walking upstairs to his stash. He hadn't bothered to go into the basement to smoke for a long time now. How could she bring a baby into a life like this?

Spence felt like a douche. No amount of smoking, pills, or beer would make him feel better. He'd sold his kids. He'd bailed on his wife and their baby-to-be. He'd checked out of life. He opened a random bottle, and with every sip of beer, he popped another pill until every last pill was gone.

As he dosed himself way over the limit, he took out pen and paper. He wanted to write a letter to the boys, to Bettina. To explain. But what could he say? There was no reason for any of this except his own damn cowardly lame-ass self. Still, he wrote.

"To my family. Bettina you have been a wonderful wife. I don't deserve you. You and the baby are better off without me. The house is paid for so at least you don't have to worry about that. Please tell my boys and the baby, tell them, well I hope the baby thrives. You'll find someone else. My boys, your dad is a very sick man. Promise me you will never drink liquor. You have it in your genes. You are cursed with a predisposition to abuse all kinds of substances. My father, the grandfather you never met, died from alcohol abuse, just as I am dying now from an overdose. Don't let anyone kid you, prescription drugs, drugs your doctor prescribes, can kill you. Please don't party in college. I hope you never have to suffer the depression…"

Spence dropped the pen and fell to the floor.

Downstairs Bettina heard a thump and lumbered to her feet. She walked up the steps dreading what she'd find. Vomit. A half-conscious husband who had actually checked out a long time ago. Then she saw him. His lips were blue. She leaned over him. Barely breathing. She saw the note paper, noticed his handwriting, saw the pill bottles, the liquor bottle. God, please, no.

Scared and angry, she forced herself to pick up one of the sheets of stationary. "…your grandfather," she read, her eyes glazing over with unshed tears. Spence had never talked about his family. Certainly he had never mentioned a grandfather.

She roused herself, picked up his cell phone where it had fallen along with him, and called 9-1-1.

It took forever to give the operator all the information she requested. "Can't you hang up and call the hospital? He's dying. I need them now."

"Ma'am, emergency medical services are on their way. I'm staying on the line with you to make sure we have everything we need in place when they admit him to the hospital. Go over the timeline for me. Can you do that?"

Bettina didn't hear sirens, and that scared her. She threw the phone down and tried to shake Spence awake, but he didn't respond. He was already dead. She knew it.

She picked up the phone and screamed into it. "He's dead. It's too late."

"Ma'am, please, listen to me."

She tried to breath, to listen through the roar in her head. There wasn't anything else to do.

"What position is he in? Have you moved him? We

got cut off there for a minute. Is he still on his stomach?"

"Yes."

"No vomit?"

"No." She thought she heard a faint siren. "I think I hear sirens."

"Are you on a portable phone? Where are you in the house?"

"Yes, I was upstairs, but I'm going to the front door now."

"Good. You did good. Are the emergency personnel on premises?"

Bettina just said a hasty thank you and opened the door. She pointed up the stairs as two uniformed men rushed toward her. Then she fainted.

She woke up in the ambulance, next to Spence. God in heaven. "He's not…"

"He's still with us, ma'am. We didn't want to leave you in your condition, so this was the best we can do."

She and her belly squeezed into the ambulance, but the men managed efficiently even as the horn blared as they passed through an intersection. The truck swayed, and she thought she'd be sick. Both med techs were working on Spence. She couldn't see what they were doing, but she gagged when she smelled his vomit. He'd live another day, but she'd give him hell for it.

****

The next day dawned sunny and even prettier than the day before. The boys played on the beach, only stopping for a picnic lunch of PBJ sandwiches. Chloe read a mystery novel. Her mom was making them dinner tonight, all the boys' favorites. Chocolate cake, also a favorite of Chloe's. What the boys called "potato salad" but really consisted of boiled potatoes with Italian dressing poured over them. She'd also make the real thing, with mayo and chopped eggs and celery, for her and Chloe. Hot dogs would round out the menu. Since moving to Blue Lake, her mother had learned how to grill.

At four o'clock Chloe forced the boys from the water. They cleaned up and put on fresh clothes. The bungalow was adorable. She had Eva's old room, and the boys bunked across the hall. Someone had stocked the fridge and pantry before they'd arrived. The kindnesses Eva and Wanda had shown made her wish that she never had to leave. Leaving her mother would be most painful of all. She was losing her place in the world. But maybe a better place waited for her and her children. Like Seattle.

The boys yelled they were ready to go, and Chloe snapped out of her fog. They piled into the car, and she made sure they fastened their seat belts and soon were heading down the cute little Main Street, with a bank, summer shops, and Fast Eddie's where she'd ordered the best hamburger of her entire life. She'd love to come here and just spend a day shopping. She didn't have any beachy clothes. They hadn't fit into her life before. And the store windows had enticing glimpses of pretty pastel cover-ups and gorgeous jeweled sandals.

She could even get a pedicure and manicure at the little spa in town. Maybe tomorrow morning. Josh and Tommy had begged to spend the night with Grandma and had packed their own backpacks with pjs and toothbrushes.

The kids piled out and ran into Grandma's kitchen, where cookies came fresh from the oven and Grandma let them have one before dinner.

"The cottage looks charming, Mom." Chloe studied the changes to the summer home they'd had for many years. The old wicker furniture was gone. Mom's good stuff showed better here than back at the old house. The familiar feel of the framed photos and knickknacks made Chloe nostalgic for simpler days.

They sat for dinner at the table Chloe had sat at for meals since she could remember, ate the food she always remembered eating and adoring. The boys were full of stories for their grandma, and her mother chatted happily about her new life in Blue Lake.

"You should let a Realtor take you around," her mother said. "Not for now, but some day, maybe. There are some bigger places that are just darling. You know Daniel has restored a good part of the town's historic district. Those places might be a little pricey, but they are gorgeous."

"Mommy, yes," Josh begged. "Let's move here instead of Seattle."

Her mother raised an eyebrow.

Chloe mouthed a snotty "thank you" to her mother over the boys' heads. Stop it, she told herself. She didn't want to ruin this vacation with ill-chosen words. Her mom was hurting. Chloe understood that.

Chloe pulled the new Pirates video out of her purse and looked at her mother. Her mom nodded.

"Boys, why don't you watch the video while Grandma and I set the table?"

"I'm sorry my new job's in Seattle, Mom." Her mother handed Chloe familiar dinner plates from a new cupboard. Chloe set the table. "I couldn't turn it down. I have two boys to raise on my own. I need to make a living wage, and those kind of jobs are just not here in Michigan right now. I had to make a tough decision."

Her mother nodded and laid silverware next to each plate.

"How did the boys react when you told them?"

"Josh wasn't happy at first, but now they think it's an adventure. We get to live by the ocean." Chloe didn't mention the family meltdown while packing.

"But right here in Blue Lake you have water. Lots of it."

Chloe nodded. It was beautiful here. Seattle seemed a long way away. It would be hard to leave her mother. "You'll come to Seattle for Christmas and stay the winter." Not a question. "Stay a month. Two. As long as you'd like. I'm decorating a room just for you. I'll buy you a Seattle car."

She and her mom had formed such a winning team raising the boys after the divorce. She wanted to believe her mother would come west for good eventually.

"I'll just put these dogs on the grill," her mom said. But then on her way out to the tiny patio, she turned. "And you're sure this is not about me moving to Blue Lake? You don't feel like I abandoned you?"

"No, Mom, honest. It's not that. I'm going where the money and the work lead me. That's all."

"Well." Her mom wielded the hot dog fork. "I wanted us to each stand on her own feet. I moved away first. I guess I can't complain when you do the same."

"Mom, I will miss you every single day." It was true. "I'll come and stay at Blue Heaven every summer. You can close up the house here and winter with us."

"That's what I tried to stop. The way we depend on each other. I wanted you to have your own life. Find a man. Have that daughter you've always dreamed of."

"You mean granddaughter you've always wanted."

They laughed quietly.

"We'll work it out," her mom said.

"I know we will."

"Maybe you'll meet someone out there."

"I want to, Mom. I'm ready."

"You mean you're lonely."

"Yes." She tried not to think about Luke. Tried to believe there was someone better out there for her.

****

Chloe had the bungalow to herself. As usual, a bonfire raged outside, but she didn't join in. It wasn't the same without the boys. She sat on the big front porch, the murmur of voices at the bonfire a soothing background noise as she watched the waning moon reflected in the dark water of Lake Huron.

"Hey," a voice said. Luke. She turned to see him on the porch, standing there.

"Hey," she said. She'd wondered if she'd run into him up here, but it never occurred to her that he'd seek her out. He'd never called her in the weeks after he'd left, and she'd been alone in Sterling Pines. Now here he stood.

"I thought the boys might be watching the Tigers."

"Oh." So he hadn't come to see her, but her boys. So sweet. "They're staying with Grandma tonight." He stood at the edge of the porch. "Have a seat if you want to."

Luke took a chair next to her.

They were both quiet for a while, just gazing out at the lake, breathing in the good air, gazing at the hundreds of stars in the sky.

Chloe wondered why Luke was here. She didn't think he'd really come to watch baseball with her boys at all. "Did your mom send you over here at my mom's request?"

"No, why would you think that?"

To talk her out of Seattle. But she didn't say that. She was just happy that her mother had kept her promise and had not said anything to Wanda about her move.

"I can't imagine why else you'd be here." Her voice caught, and her throat burned with the words. Wow. She was surprised that she was this emotional about him still. She had to get over that.

"I wanted to see you. And the boys."

"You don't date single moms. Remember?"

"For a long time I had a rule a about single moms. Then I met you. And Josh and Tommy."

Chloe held her breath. Was he—did he—he couldn't be—

"I'm ready to break that rule," Luke said.

Chloe exhaled. For thousands of minutes, she'd waited to hear those words. She had called herself every kind of fool for wishing and hoping he'd say them. And now, he had.

"If you're okay with that?" He started to get up from his chair. Chloe couldn't think straight. Her thoughts swirled around. She was more than okay with Luke wanting to date her, but in the mix, Seattle waited. She should tell him.

"What're you guys talking about?" Luke sank back into his seat as Finn, one of the locals she'd met last night, came around the corner from the bonfire onto the porch. He made himself at home on another rocker on the other side of Chloe. "Hey, I'm Finn."

"Yeah, we met last night. Chloe."

"Luke and I also saw you with Eva Bryman at Fast Eddie's last night. Before the bonfire."

"Oh." Chloe's heart missed a beat. Luke had been watching her when she hadn't known it. Is that when he'd decided to break his rule for her?

"Nice night," Finn said.

Luke made a disgusted noise.

"How long you up here for, Chloe?"

"My boys and I are just here for a week." But Chloe wondered now if everything had changed. Would she stay here if Luke asked? What about the job? She fought an internal battle while Finn continued to talk and Luke continued to glower at Finn. What was happening here? Luke? Jealous?

"Oh, that's right. You have kids. Where are they?"

"Staying with their grandma tonight."

"Chloe's mom has a cottage on Sparrow Street," Luke said.

Finn ignored Luke and kept talking to Chloe. "I should bring my nephew by tomorrow to meet them. He's seven."

"That would be great." Chloe said. "They get bored when it's just the two of them all the time."

"We could go for a spin in my boat," Finn said.

"They'd love that," Chloe said, although she hated boating. It made her seasick.

"Great. Let's say noon?"

"That sounds fine." She'd do anything she could to make this last week in Blue Lake special for her boys.

"Finn's got a speed boat. The lake gets pretty choppy," Luke said.

Chloe felt out of her depth. There were too many undercurrents, and she wasn't even in the boat yet. She made idle polite conversation and hoped Finn would leave soon so she could find out exactly how Luke wanted to break his rule. She asked Finn how he got the day off in the middle of the week.

"I'm on vacation. The best part of living in Blue Lake is that when you get a week off, you don't have to go anywhere."

"More like six months," Luke said.

By the light of the porch, Chloe saw a shadow of regret flit across Luke's face right after the words came out of his mouth. He glanced at Finn.

Finn looked pained. "Actually, I'm laid off right now. I'm a construction electrician, and there's just no work in the state for us right now, construction being at a total standstill."

"You'll find something, buddy," Luke said, clearly trying to make up for dissing his friend.

"I recently had a bout of unemployment myself," Chloe said.

"Did you find something?" Luke asked.

Chloe knew this was the time to tell Luke about Seattle, or it would be, except she couldn't risk it. Couldn't risk him talking her out of leaving.

"Don't you have to go now?" Luke asked Finn.

"No." He shook Luke's hand off his shoulder.

Chloe watched Luke lay claim to her. At least that's what it felt like and also sweetly delicious to be wanted by him, by Luke.

She missed whatever the guys said to each other, their tones low. But Finn got up and said good-bye, promising to bring his nephew by with the boat tomorrow for a day of fishing.

"What should I get for my boys? Fishing poles? Life jackets? Bait?"

"Not a thing," Finn said. Then he regarded Luke. "You're welcome to come along, Luke."

"Great. I'll take you up on that."

Chloe's body relaxed. She hadn't known she'd been tense, but she hated boating. With Luke there, the boys would be safe. She somehow knew this in her heart.

"This is embarrassing." Chloe spoke lower than usual so both men had to lean in to hear her. "I am afraid of boating. But my boys love it."

"What's to fear?" Finn swore he'd handle the boat with care.

"It's not that. I trust you." She said the words to Finn, but her eyes were locked on Luke's. "I get seasick and also have a panic issue." It took everything she had to admit that she'd have to take medication to get on a silly little fishing boat.

"I'll take good care of your boys. You can check out the town. There's a lady place." Luke furrowed his brow. "Spa. And shopping. That kind of stuff."

"Thank you!" She wanted to kiss Luke. Her boys would be safe with him, and she could go into town and have a girly day.

Luke loved the way the moonglow touched Chloe's face, giving her face a pretty sheen that reminded him of pearls. Even without the moonlight, she had a lovely face. And of course her awesome body, which naturally Finn had picked up on.

"Your friend seems nice," she said.

"He's not," Luke replied before thinking. "I mean,

yeah, he's a nice guy, but he loves the summer women. Loves to get what he can, if you know what I mean."

Chloe didn't say anything, but he could tell she was thinking about what he'd said.

"I'm not like that," Luke clarified.

"I'm glad you're going fishing with them," Chloe said. "I would not have done a spa day if it was just Finn and his nephew, because Josh and Tommy don't know them. But the boys will feel comfortable with you there. You're a big deal to them, you know."

The noises of the bonfire party breaking up reached them. Luke knew his mother or Eva would lock up the office at midnight so that guests wouldn't take the party upstairs into the social area right above her quarters.

So, it must be getting close to midnight, Luke thought. All was calm. Except his heart, which beat so loud he figured Chloe could hear it.

"It's late," Chloe said, standing.

"And we're here alone." Luke stood and took a step toward her. She seemed a little nervous, but she didn't back away from him, so he took another step forward, then another. Then he kissed her.

What was she doing? Chloe kissed Luke, hungry for his taste, a taste she remembered like it was yesterday. Mint toothpaste and moonlight. She heard the waves rushing against the shore, and she rushed like the waves, crashing against him, diving deeper into the kiss.

Then she stopped thinking.

After one long kiss lead to the next, Luke took her hand and opened the front door that led directly into the living room.

She pulled him past the sofa, into the bedroom

she'd slept alone in last night, wishing he was there with her. She admitted it. She wanted him. That simple. He obviously wanted her, too. Was this love? She loved him, she must, or maybe it was only lust. Because lust overwhelmed her at the moment.

She'd be gone in a week, and this might be her only chance to find out if her love for Luke was real. She wouldn't risk sleeping in the same room with Luke when the boys were here. But now, the moon had conspired with the sun to get the two of them here, alone, together. And she would not say no to that fortunate alignment of the stars. Her heart wouldn't let her. She'd tell Luke about Seattle later. Once he knew he couldn't live without her. They'd deal with it then. Lots of people worked out long-distance relationships. Or he could move with her. People needed yard work in Seattle, too.

He moved her hair aside and kissed her softly on her neck. The new sensation made her moan. She pushed all thought away. This was just for her. She needed to feel loved. And Luke made her feel loved right now, with his tender kisses and possessive embrace.

She shed any inhibition she'd felt with their easily discarded summer clothes. She lay open to his hungry gaze. So good to be cared for in this way, to be loved, to be worshipped for who she was, underneath the masks and layers she put on in public.

Luke, not a man of many words on a normal day, but now, here, he didn't have to talk to send her body the signal that he wanted her with a deeply thrilling passion. His hardness against her thigh told her, and she moved her hand to wrap him with greedy fingers. She breathed in his scent, the fresh water smell mixed with newly mown lawn that clung to his body even when his clothes were off.

He sighed when she touched him, taking her invitation to cup her breasts and kiss her lips. She lost herself in a dizzy whirl of emotion she couldn't name or trace. Almost breathless, she broke the kiss to press her lips against his neck, letting her tongue feel the deliciousness of his suntanned skin.

If she could bury herself in the crook of his neck forever, she'd be happy to die there, so beloved, so cared for. Luke had broken his rule for her. Somehow they would bring their love into the light of day, just by the things they did with each other now, with a silent moonlight promise.

She closed her eyes as they melted into each other. She could follow him anywhere, like they were dancing an ancient dance, and each movement brought them closer and closer together. They could be making a baby together. That thought made her eyes pop open. Her body stilled under him.

As attuned as he was to her every movement, she froze, and he opened his eyes right into hers. He knew what they'd done, too. He stopped, still inside her. Skin to skin. She'd discovered that she could make him lose himself so completely that he forgot all common sense. And the same could be said of her.

She grabbed him with her hands, one on each cheek. "No. Don't go. It's fine."

He laughed a low, wicked laugh, kissing her neck again just under her ear, reestablishing a smooth rhythm, stroking against her, enflaming her beyond the point of holding back anymore. So she didn't. She let the rich waves move through her body as a sound rose from her belly, a sound of pleasure fulfilled as lap after lap of primal emotion engulfed her.

Her own throbbing set him free. She squeezed her pelvic muscles to hug him tightly and wrapped her arms around his waist. He lowered himself and cradled her as they rolled side to side and looked at each other.

"You're dangerous." His whisper in her ear thrilled her. Nobody had ever called her dangerous before. She liked it. "Are you on the pill?"

"No." Her laugh escaped before she could catch it. "I have no need to be. Or I didn't. For a long time. Until tonight." She moved even closer, so that their bodies touched all the way to their toes. "It's not the right time of the month."

She rested there, her head on his shoulder. He kept his arm around her as he reached on the floor for his jeans. He pulled out a foil wrapped condom. Wow. Spence had never been able to go twice in one night. Not even on their honeymoon. She peeked down. Stone hard and already rolling on the condom. "Let's not tempt Mother Nature too much," he said.

Chapter Eleven

Spence woke up in an unfamiliar bed. His head ached, his teeth hurt, his body, cold with sweat, didn't make sense, except…except when he was in detox. His queasy stomach made him turn over and open his eyes. A twin bed. Painted white cement walls. Not a jail cell, but might as well be. Back in rehab. Again.

After dry heaving over the toilet bowl for what seemed like hours, he struggled to recall what had brought him here, but it was all black. No memories, just a sense of sickening dread and his dark familiar friend, depression.

"He's up!" a nurse in a uniform of kitten pants and top informed the room.

"Where's my wife? Why am I here? What happened to me?"

His boys were gone. He'd see them again, maybe once a year if he was lucky. The baby! God help him. He had to get better for the baby. And for Bettina. But as the nurse took his vital signs and he fought off nausea, he knew it wouldn't work if he got sober for anyone except himself.

The nurse hadn't answered any of his questions, but he heard his wife's voice and struggled to his feet. He wore a horrible hospital johnny, but it hardly mattered. Clearly something much worse than showing his ass was happening here.

It stayed like that. Hot, then cold. Burning and shivering and itching. Shit and dry heaves. More than once he wished he'd died. This seemed to go on forever. No day or night, no soothing sleep, only nightmares. He was still being given medication, but it didn't help. He'd heard Bettina's voice that one time but didn't see her until they had a meeting with an addiction specialist.

Dr. Michaels would keep Bettina off his back. He hoped. It was all he could do to walk down the hall supported by an attendant. He still couldn't remember why he was here. The attendant opened Dr. Michaels's door, and Bettina sat there, shredded tissue in hand, eyes red of rim. *Oh God, give me the strength to deal with this woman*, he prayed. He had never been a big fan of Jesus, but when things got this bad, praying helped. Apparently God didn't hold it against you if you didn't quite believe in him.

He took his seat. Stole a look at his wife.

"Hi, honey."

She wouldn't turn her face to his.

"I'm sorry." He wasn't sure what he was sorry for. Clearly he'd ODed. But why? How? When? He might as well get his all-inclusive apologies out of the way. He felt so sick and tired he wanted most of all to go back to his cot and four walls, curl into a ball, and breathe. Or not.

She still didn't glance his way. She didn't speak. Fine.

Dr. Michaels glanced over a chart.

"This is something you wrote last time you were here," the doc said. Spence didn't remember ever writing anything while in rehab. He slumped in his chair. Whatever came, he wouldn't like it.

He was right.

"Does Bettina know about your family situation? Your family of origin?"

Spence shrugged. He wasn't sure. Actually, he was pretty sure he hadn't mentioned it. He didn't like to think about that stuff.

"They live in Iowa. I've never met them. Spence hates them."

No. They were not going to make him talk about that.

"Have you ever been curious about why he hates his folks?"

"They're not my 'folks.'" Spence's legs did a little dance of their own. He tried to make them stop, but they wouldn't. "We don't talk about them."

"Why don't you tell your wife—"

"Soon to be ex if you don't start talking. Now." Bettina finally spoke.

Ex. Oh, no, not again. At least this time he'd have warning and not come home to an empty house, no wife, no kids. No clothes in Chloe's closet, no toothbrush in her holder, no jewelry box on her dresser. She'd left a few of the kids' things behind, but she'd taken their beds. She'd left his to lie in alone.

"I, ah, what?" His hands were shaking. He couldn't think. Wait. Think. Remember. "Oh, wait, no, don't leave, please, let me think, I just need a sec." His mind blanked.

"Your parents."

"Oh, those people. They adopted me when I was ten. I was abandoned as a baby, orphaned. Foster care for ten years. Then they needed help on the farm, more help than foster care allowed ten-year-olds, so they adopted me. I was your basic slave laborer." He turned to face Bettina and stuck his tongue out. Then he realized what he'd done and slammed his hand over his mouth. "Jesus, I'm sorry, I didn't mean to do that, oh God, don't leave. I love you."

Bettina hadn't said a word. She clutched her rounded belly.

"It's okay." The doc turned to Bettina. "Some of Spence's motor skills are out of sync. He'll be fine, we think. But it may take some time for him to settle down."

"He's behaving like a ten-year-old." Bettina said it and then he saw realizing dawn. She'd made the connection. "In one of your suicide notes, you mentioned you had an alcoholic grandfather. Does that mean you found your family of origin? We have medical records?"

Spence swayed in his chair. Too many questions. She asked too many questions. Finally the doc spoke. *Thanks, Doc. Saved me.*

"Yes, something shifted for Spence at age ten. Spence, you wrote out your history for me here, last time. I'm sorry to see you back again and with the circumstances so similar."

"How do you mean?" Bettina massaged her back and talked to the doctor.

"It's better if you and Spence can have this conversation where you both feel supported. I'm the silent support. Talk to your husband. Tell him how you feel."

"Well, I hate him," she told the doctor.

"That's fine, but tell him, not me."

Spence put his hand over his eyes. *Why was he such a fuck up? So he'd been an orphan, so his family hadn't wanted him, so he was adopted, so he had to work hard, so the fuck what?*

Bettina slapped the hand from his eyes. He flinched.

"What? Don't worry. I won't say it again. I know you heard." Bettina looked pissed as hell, tapping her foot like his adoptive mother used to do. He closed his eyes and tried to remember, but there were a lot of blanks. "Say something, asshole."

He closed his eyes and reached out a hand to the doctor. "Could you let me see those pages?" The doc handed them over.

Spence scanned. "No idea who natural parents were slash are. No idea of medical history." He remembered that now. It wasn't in the pages. He put them down. He didn't want to see what else he'd written. "Chloe got so angry she hired a guy to find my parents. My real parents. Good ol' dad was dead, but he had a sister who gave us the medical information. My mom had been thirteen. Raped. Hid it. Had the baby, well, had me, outside, alone, and put it, ah, put me, in a purse, an old purse. She tried to keep me in her room, but her mother saw and took me to some Catholic Sisters of Mercy or some such adoption people. I was not adopted as an infant. I already knew that."

"Did you meet your mother?" For the first time Bettina's voice softened a little.

"She thought it best to leave the past in the past." True story. He got so hot, sweat beaded up all over his body, making him cold. He shivered. The doc had a thin hospital blanket on a side chair, and he nodded toward it.

"Go ahead," he said. "Get it if you need it."

What he needed. What he needed. "I need you." Spence blurted to Bettina as he got up on shaky bare legs to retrieve the blanket. He wrapped himself in it. "I know I'm not supposed to say that." He directed his comment to the doctor. "But I'm being honest, right? I need her. I need my boys, too. My family means everything to me. I never had one, not really. Those people didn't love me. I was a paycheck."

"Now I'm YOUR paycheck."

Boy, she knew how to bust his balls. Wasn't there a heart beating inside her enormous breast? The room started to telescope, and then everything went black.

****

Bettina had been checked over by her OB and released the same day. She had to call one of the teachers she liked best to come get her. The woman had wanted to know what had happened, where was Spence, was she okay? Bettina played it off. Oh sure, everything's fine, Spence had to go out of town on business and she'd had a cramp and didn't feel she should drive, so she'd called a cab. Silly.

She'd learned how to lie from Spence. She got pretty good at it. When she got home, she trudged up the steps, grabbing up the pages Spence had written. She took them into the bedroom with her, sat on the bed with her swollen feet up, and read.

What she saw, self-indulgent bullshit. He wasn't thinking of her or the baby. He wasn't thinking of his sons. He only thought "poor me." Well, to hell with him. Bettina understood why Chloe had taken her children and left Spence. Now she had to decide.

Would she do the same?

It was tempting. She had a good job. Her mother lived in Arizona, but hell, she could afford quality daycare. A nanny. It wasn't what they'd planned, but life didn't work like that. She let tears roll down but didn't bother to break into sobs. The jerk wasn't worth it. He obviously didn't feel she and their child were worth living for.

What a line of crap she'd fed herself when she'd first met him. Oh, Mr. Wonderful, Mr. Misunderstood. She had wanted to take care of the broken man she'd married. Yes, a bad time for real estate in Detroit, he'd get back on his feet someday. But for the first few months, hell, years, she'd done all she could to make it up to the wounded child inside Spence. Then he started acting like a druggie teenager, and she'd started to become annoyed. As his behavior escalated, she got scared. Her OB had told her she must keep calm in these final weeks. No matter what stress her husband was under, she must make herself her first priority.

She could do that. She'd seen Spence do it for years. Her first act of rebellion was falling asleep in her clothes without turning down the bed first. She slept like a child, but she woke up a woman with some decisions to make.

Should she call Chloe?

Oh so tempting. With a mix of horror and chagrin, she realized Chloe was her only friend. Unless you counted what's-her-name from the Al-Anon group. Suzy. Bettina dragged herself out of bed, stripped, and stood under the hot shower. She had to get the smell of hospital off her. While the water pounded down, she admitted something. She was no different from Suzy or any of the other people at Al-Anon. And admitting that became a first step into a new reality for Bettina.

What had Suzy said? "Get out while you can." Bettina would certainly take that under advisement.

****

Luke woke up in Chloe's bed, her warm body cuddled in his arms. He froze as he heard a car pull into the gravel driveway. That would be his mother, ready to begin her work day. He knew she'd go upstairs first with the fresh muffins she'd made at home. She'd set them out with cut fruit and start the large coffee urn.

It didn't matter. She'd already seen his car in the parking lot. Unless…

"Chloe," he whispered, gently pulling his arm out from under her shoulders. She stirred and her beautiful eyes opened an inch. "My mom's here."

She jumped out of bed without a word while he quietly zipped his jeans. Man, she looked good naked with her sleepy eyes and hair all messed up. He wished he could pull her right back into bed, but that wasn't going to happen.

"I'll just say I got here early to pick up the boys for the fishing trip."

"Right."

Chloe reached for her robe. They could both hear his mom upstairs, getting ready for the guests who didn't feel like using their own cottage kitchenettes this early in the day.

Chloe headed for the bathroom. Luke finished dressing and started out toward the kitchen, wishing he at least had a toothbrush. As he walked past the bathroom, Chloe opened the door and thrust a toothbrush with a dollop of toothpaste on it at him.

He brushed his teeth at the kitchen sink and hid the toothbrush in Chloe's room in the bedside table, right next to the condoms. Crap. His mother would be emptying the wastebasket in here and yep, there was his condom, right on top of the basket. He heard her steps coming down the stairs, so he grabbed the wicker basket and knocked on the bathroom door. The running shower reminded him he needed to take a piss. Really bad.

He opened the door and stuck the wastebasket in the center of the room. He just made it into the kitchen when his mother knocked on the locked door that separated the office from the bungalow's living quarters. She had a key, but she wouldn't just let herself in when a guest was using the bungalow. She wouldn't even normally knock this early but would wait for Chloe and the boys to head down to the beach before she vacuumed and changed sheets. She must know he was here. Of course. She'd seen his truck.

"Luke?"

"Morning, Mom." He opened the door.

"You're here early." She walked into the kitchen.

"Finn and I are taking the boys fishing this morning. As usual he's running a little late."

His mother said nothing. She stared at his bare feet and bed hair. He wasn't fooling her. Not for one minute. He shrugged.

She shook her head and tried to hide her smile. He bet she'd be on the phone to Ursula the minute she could manage it.

****

Four days after their first session, Bettina sat with Spence in front of Dr. Michaels's desk. The doctor wrote a prescription for a pill that would make him sick if he had a drop of alcohol. He pushed it toward them, and Bettina grabbed it.

"You are not my mother, okay? I can fill my own damn prescriptions." Truth, he wanted to hold the script. He got an anticipatory surge just seeing the square of paper.

For a week, he had done a detox in the hospital. He had been fortunate—well, he still didn't feel fortunate, but he worked on that—Bettina had found him and called 9-1-1 before the pills he'd taken had completely engulfed his system. But now there would be no marijuana, medical or otherwise. There would be no uppers or downers. There would just be this one pill.

The doctor checked his notes. "You need sixty days, not six."

"I've done this all before. It never worked then. Why should it now?"

Bettina sat rigid beside him, the prescription slip clutched in her hand. She had not met his eyes, even once. Spence sighed. He took Bettina's hand. The one not holding the prescription. She let him.

"Listen. I'm getting clean for good. That's it. I had my party, and it's not over. It's just going to be a sober party this time."

She slowly turned toward him. "You're not the only one who has been down this road before," she said. "You cannot promise you'll never fall off the cliff again."

"It's a wagon." Spence attempted a weak joke.

"In your case, it's a high steep cliff, Grand Canyon size."

She shook her head, but he thought he detected a

slight smile trying to work its way onto her face. He did not deserve this woman. He knew she would never walk away from him like Chloe had.

"Look, I wouldn't blame you if you hated me. I hate myself. And if you want me to, I will stay sixty days. But Chloe is taking the boys to Seattle, and I need to stop her somehow."

"Why did you agree to it in the first place? She'd have needed your permission to take them out of state."

Bettina didn't miss a trick. Shrewd mind behind that sweet face. He'd have to own up at some point. Might as well be now. "I did it for you. For us."

Nobody spoke for a full minute. Spence couldn't bear it, the avoiding, the hiding, the lies. It had to be over. For his own good. For himself. Or there might not be any more of him—the good dad, the nice husband, the sincere person—left.

Bettina just waited for him to finish answering. The doctor, too, clearly expected him to continue.

"She signed the house over to me. Paid off the mortgage."

"What are you talking about?"

"She gave me clear title."

"I thought the house was yours?"

"I liked you thinking that. It made me feel less of a loser." He got a hit of relief for having come clean. Swiftly followed by dread. Bettina's face paled. Her body shrunk from his side even more. She stared at the wall, not at him.

"What else?" When she finally spoke, she looked him in the eye. He saw fury there. And hurt.

"That's it. I swear."

"It's more than enough. You could have killed

yourself. You tried to…" She choked back a sob as he watched her carefully controlled façade fall apart.

Yes. Bald truth. But if he thought Bettina might take pity on him because of his suicide attempt, he now knew that wasn't going to happen. Just another delusion.

She smacked him on his arm, and then she did it again. The doctor coughed and raised one finger as if to say "time out."

"Bettina." The doctor waited while she swiped away tears. She nodded and Spence knew she was ready to listen. "Will you tell Spence why you want to hit him?"

She put her hands in her face, and her shoulders shook as she silently wept. He had done this to her. Devastated, he tried to keep up with his wife's actions and emotions. To not break down himself. He had to be strong for her.

She sniffed and accepted a tissue from the doctor. "Because he would rather be dead than have a life with me and our baby. He'd rather be dead than do without his precious drugs and alcohol."

She ripped at her tissue, not meeting Spence's eyes. He grabbed for her hand, but she snatched it away. "Baby, that's just not true!"

"What is the truth, Spence?" The doctor held the box of tissue toward him as his eyes penetrated through every defense he'd built up.

Spence touched his face. Wet. Him? Crying? He didn't think so. Tears fell. Strange. He couldn't remember the last time he'd cried.

"I didn't want…I couldn't stop. I wanted to be a good person. For a long time, I didn't realize I was an addict. Doctors gave me pills. That made it okay."

"You doctor shopped. Used more than one pharmacy. You had to know that's wrong. And what about your alcohol use?"

"That's what I mean!" Spence's head wound tight as a vice grip. "Wouldn't you want to kill yourself if you were in my shoes?"

Bettina began a fresh round of sobs. He wanted his pipe so bad. That was the difference between them. She let it all out, he kept it all stowed inside. Unless his body betrayed him, like with the silent tears.

The doctor wore a pissed expression Spence knew well. "If I had a beautiful, intelligent wife and a new baby on the way? Of course I wouldn't want to kill myself. You have everything to live for."

"No!" Spence was not going to let this guy railroad him. Nobody understood. Not one person. "If you were a fucked-up mess who never saw his kids, got money for giving them up, lived off women, never even tried to work…getting high was my full-time job, if you were me, you'd get why I did it."

"Let me suggest you change the picture a bit. Look toward the future, not back at the past. Lay it to rest." The doctor's face had softened a fraction.

"But I don't want them to go!" In that moment, Spence knew he would do anything to keep his kids close.

"Then I'd say you had quite a mess to clean up before your next child arrives, don't you?"

Chapter Twelve

When Chloe got out of the shower, she heard Luke talking to his mom in the kitchen. She saw the wastebasket in the middle of the floor and knew immediately what that was about. She smiled, wrapped the used condoms in tissue, and put the wad into the pocket of her robe. She'd discard the evidence later. Then she blew her hair dry and put on her makeup.

She went through the hall and closed her bedroom door without greeting Wanda. Usually, Wanda stayed in the office and upstairs. She didn't come into Chloe's area of the house until she was sure of the timing. And yet, this morning, there she sat, in the kitchen, at the table, taking a coffee break. Chloe had seen all this from the corner of her eye as she went from the bathroom to the bedroom.

What was that all about?

Her cell rang before she even finished dressing. Her mother.

"I hear Luke is taking the boys fishing this morning," her mom said.

"Uh-huh."

"They're still sleeping."

Chloe checked the time. A bit after eight.

"What time did you have them up until?"

"We watched late night TV. Then they were too wound up to sleep, so we put in a movie.

"Well, Finn's not here yet, so let them sleep."

"But Luke's there. My friend Alice saw his truck parked at your place at 5 a.m. this morning. And Carrie said his truck was parked there at 2 a.m. when Fast Eddie's closed."

Chloe let her mother come to her own conclusions. She didn't deny, and she didn't admit. After she hung up the phone, she sat on the bed and let the sadness she'd been trying to push away since the day her boss had manhandled her take over. Why was it rushing out now? Was this about last night? About what happened and why it happened, and the fact that if it was ever going to happen again, she'd have to tell Luke about Seattle. She dreaded telling him but prayed they'd be able to work out some kind of long-distance commitment. Well, unless that wasn't part of his plan. Unless she was just a one night girl. But she didn't think Luke played that game. For one thing, he would not choose a single mom for a fling.

****

Luke smiled a silly smile. He couldn't wipe it off his face. The boys were having a great time. Finn was good to Zak, his only nephew. He had a way of being easy with the boys that Luke took cues from. Luke had not really been around young boys much, well, not since he'd been one.

He put worms on their hooks, untangled their lines, got them juice boxes from the cooler, reminded them to put sunscreen on. He helped the three boys while Finn fished in a few spots they knew along the lake, inlets where they could catch bass and perch. So they were used to being quiet with each other. They were also used to drinking more beer, but Finn's sister had contemplated the six pack in the cooler and removed two of the beers.

Chloe had done something similar. She'd checked and rechecked the boys' canvas bag that held towels and sunscreen and two small pair of sunglasses. The boys refused to wear the sunglasses, and they had to be forced to apply sunscreen. They hated it, Chloe had warned him.

Meanwhile, she'd thanked Finn sweetly for bringing the picnic lunch and the extra poles, and for including her boys in such a fun day. Luke, who hoped he had rocked her night world, got a quick kiss on the cheek when her boys weren't looking. Finn must wonder about that, but, a stroke of luck, he knew better than to bring it up with the little guys around. What would he say to Finn? That he and Chloe were taking it slow? He wasn't sure if that was true for her, but for him, absolutely true. He'd like to take their relationship to the next step, even though it meant breaking his number one rule, which Finn knew about, and would not hesitate to use.

"Uncle Finn," Zak said, "can we go swimming?"

"What? Tired of fishing already?"

"We'll fish some more later after we swim," Josh promised.

"Might as well let them swim before we eat," Luke said.

"Okay, but you all have to wear life jackets."

A chorus of complaints, but eventually they all zipped into jackets while Finn navigated the boat next to a sandbar at an inlet only the locals knew existed.

The boys jumped into the water, and Finn handed Luke a beer. They both faced the three bobbing heads in the water. Both kept constant count through the splashing and screeching. Alive and content on a beautiful day, not a cloud in the blue, blue sky, the water full of ripples and splashes and laughter.

Then Finn erased Luke's good mood by saying, "So you've got a thing for another single mother. Don't you ever learn?"

He shook his head. "I guess not."

"Word is you spent the night."

Damn small towns. Everybody knew everything all the time.

"Why would you want to do that? After the last time, you moped around for months."

Years was more like it. He still got mopey every Christmas when he took out the ornament that Bella had made him in preschool. A little foam coffee cup, a red pipe cleaner through the bottom shaped like an ornament hook, and silver glitter rimming the top of the cup, so that turned upside down it resembled a Christmas bell.

"Chloe's different. She's worth it."

"She's hot."

"No shit."

They sipped their beer and munched on the sandwiches Finn's sister had made. Finn ripped open a bag of chips, and they took handfuls of those.

"Why, dude?"

Finn wouldn't let it go.

"I didn't mean for anything to happen. It just did."

Then the boys were climbing back into the boat demanding towels and sandwiches and chips.

"I hate bologna," Josh said.

Luke went through the cooler Chloe had packed.

Sure enough, he found a big plastic container of peanut butter crackers, which he passed around. Then Josh got the idea to put chips inside the crackers.

"These are really good, you should try them!"

So they all did. And the chip crackers tasted pretty good, Luke had to admit.

"You're a smart kid, Joshua," he said.

Josh beamed.

"Now put on some more sunscreen."

Josh's smile disappeared, but he complied, taking great pleasure in telling Tommy he had to wear some goop, too.

****

While the boys fished, Chloe went to the spa in town for some pampering. Her mother had talked her into it, and the truth was, she needed something to ground her, something physical and concrete to take her mind off Luke and Seattle and the uncertain future. Just when she thought she had it all figured out, events conspired to make chaos of her emotions.

The town consisted of one long street with a single traffic light at the center. A bank and a gas station anchored that corner, with a small grassy park on the other side of the street. On either side of the street were shops that sold beach and resort wear, sunglasses, art, pottery, candy, ice cream, fudge. Even an indie book store (sure didn't see those in Sterling Pines) and a movie theater. There were many restaurants, but Luke had told her that almost all of these businesses were only open from Memorial Day to Labor Day.

She drove along the street, past the old fashioned lamp posts with hanging baskets of pink and white petunias. She had always loved it here.

She pushed into the door of the day spa, a little surprised by the hum of activity inside when the weather was so beautiful outside. She guessed you got used to it, living here. Or, if you were a tourist, on vacation, you got a bit of pampering. That had been her plan, but now she wasn't so sure. Everyone seemed busy, and her, just a walk-in.

"Chloe?" the young woman behind a sleek column of solid blond wood asked.

"Yes," she said, surprised. How did she know her name?

"Your mom called. I'm Ginny. We live next door. It's so nice to meet you. We just love your mom."

"Oh." Chloe sort of remembered teenaged Ginny, but she'd grown up since last year. Chloe wanted anonymous for a few hours. She wanted to be alone with her thoughts, most of them about last night, but that didn't seem like it was going to happen.

"She said you wanted a mani-pedi, but let me just show you what all we have…" Ginny handed Chloe a colorful brochure with a babe in a barely-there bikini on the cover. Chloe did a double take. The babe was Ginny.

"We do a great Brazilian wax." Ginny winked.

Chloe shook her head, stunned by the choices offered. Finally, she picked a natural manicure and a reflexology pedicure.

"Ooh, good choice," Ginny said. She slide her finger through the pages of a laptop, checking the bookings. "And one of our massage ladies will be finished with her client by the time you're done with your manicure."

Ginny came from behind the desk and led Chloe

over to a manicure station. Chloe had never bothered with manicures, unlike some of her friends, who treated beauty routines like a religion, but common sense said she should pay first, so she wouldn't ruin her pretty painted nails afterward.

"Oh, didn't your mom tell you?" Gin said when she saw Chloe pulling her wallet from her purse. "Today's on her."

Chloe was pleased, hopeful that her mom had come to terms with the move. Guilt also probably rubbed Mom for not cancelling her mah-jongg game to spend the day with Chloe.

Chloe put her wallet away and turned to the wall of polish to choose her color. She normally kept her fingernails short and put pink or red polish on her toes. Today she decided, since her nails had grown out without her even noticing, that she'd splurge and do something different. "I'm going to do the pink and white French," she said to the young girl behind the manicure desk.

"I'm Jules," she said.

"I'm Chloe."

"Yeah, I know. Everybody's saying you have something going with Luke."

Jules filed Chloe's thumbnail with deep intention, and didn't look up when she spoke. Chloe froze. Cripes. Word sure got around in this town. Most likely due to her mother's wishful thinking.

"So is it true?"

Chloe was surprised—her silence didn't curb Jules's curiosity. "No. Just our mothers, wishing and hoping and making trouble." Chloe saw no reason why she had to tell a complete stranger the truth: that she was in love with Luke and had been almost since they'd met. That it was complicated, and she wasn't sure where things were going. That Luke probably needed time to trust again and time was the one thing she didn't have.

"Oh." Jules laughed. "I heard Luke's car was parked at Blue Heaven all night."

Chloe didn't have a response to that, but Jules didn't seem to need one.

By the time Jules had finished her manicure, absolutely so gorgeous that Chloe decided she'd book a regular appointment every week in Seattle, Chloe had almost forgotten that most of the women buzzing around in this spa might know more of her business than she found comfortable. Jules led her behind a sheer curtain into a room with white leather chairs, each with a built-in tub of swishing water at their base.

Someone eased Chloe's feet into the soothing water, handed her a magazine, this month's Vogue, a magazine Chloe had never in her life read, and asked if she'd like a glass of wine.

Chloe was about to decline when Eva sat down next to her. "I'd say yes. It just intensifies Naomi's genius."

"You want a glass too, Ms. Bryman?"

"Sure," Eva said.

"Naomi?"

"She's the one who does the fancy footwork, where she presses all your meridian points or whatever they are. Feels fabulous."

A different woman came with the wine and then sat at a low chair. She put a towel over her thigh and pulled one of Chloe's feet from the bath. The first person who hadn't introduced herself or started chatting right away. So restful.

Chloe took a sip of her wine, lowered her lids, slid her eyes toward Eva, who still had both her feet in the bath. After a sip of her wine, Eva asked Chloe about her new job. She didn't say "in Seattle" and, because she had a woman currently rubbing her feet with a heavenly smelling lotion, Chloe's gratitude spilled over. Seattle was a piece of news she'd have to deliver to Luke herself, and by the way things spread in this town, she should tell him sooner rather than later. Now she was sorry she'd impulsively told Eva about Seattle her first night in town after a few glasses of wine.

"I feel protective of Luke. We all do."

Chloe nodded. What had started out as a relaxing day of pampering quickly morphed into something else. "I know. And I'll talk to him about it." She felt so confused, the surface of her plan had been ruffled by Luke last night. What she didn't know is if it would go any deeper.

Naomi finished with Chloe's feet. "Excuse me for just a minute," she said, leaving Chloe and Eva alone. Chloe took that opportunity to caution Eva.

"Luke knows I have a new job, but not where. Except for my mom and the boys, you're the only person I've told. I didn't expect what happened last night, but I'm not sure it changes anything. This is the best opportunity I have for making a good life for my boys. I'm so lucky to have landed this job. I'm not going to give it up because of one night."

"It's still a man's world," Eva said.

Naomi came back with another young woman. While Naomi gave the reflexology treatment to Eva, the other girl painted Chloe's toes. She'd never been more pampered in her entire life.

Switching back into less confidential mode, Eva told Chloe about how she came up to Blue Lake after being fired from her advertising agency and how nobody thought she'd make Blue Heaven work. But she had.

"And then you met Daniel."

"Well, I actually met him the first day I came to town," Eva said. "He turned me down for a bank loan."

They both laughed.

"So does he still work at the bank?"

"No. He hated that job. His heart is in restoration. He did all the work on my bungalow. He built that airplane addition. I tell you, if he didn't love Blue Heaven so much, I'd be tempted to sell it."

"What would you rather do?"

"I keep busy. Between my mother in Florida, my college-age brother-in-law, who is home for the summer, and our new place in Georgia, I've got my hands full. Plus I want to have a baby."

"I wouldn't trade my time with my babies for anything." Chloe acknowledged that she wanted that again, wanted to stay home and care for another infant, wanted to be there when her boys came home from school. But she'd chosen another kind of life and now she had to live with it. They only had a few days left here, and there was no way Luke would step up, spring a ring on her finger, and give her everything she wanted. It was way too soon, especially for a gun-shy guy like Luke.

"I can't wait." Baby lust ignited Eva's eyes. "And I don't know what I'd do without Wanda."

"It's tough to find good help."

"Tell me again about what you do."

So Chloe explained about how she developed specialized workshops for companies who wanted to upgrade their tech skills.

"Couldn't you do that anywhere?"

Chloe had thought about being a freelancer. She'd love the flexibility, not to mention all the time she'd be able to spend with her kids. But it wasn't practical.

She shook her head. "I need health insurance and a 401K. It just isn't practical for me to freelance."

Chloe took a big breath of air. Naomi's lotion, wafting up from where she sat at Eva's feet, intoxicated her, the smell of oranges and coconut and also that underlying scent of lavender. Swoony, almost too heady. Like Luke, the man always on her mind.

The girl who painted her toe nails carefully inched Chloe's flip-flops between her toes.

"Enjoy the rest of your day," Eva said. "I'll see you later."

Chloe's heart beat fast. Freelancing would be the perfect answer if she was with Luke. All the way with him. Married to him. Ideas for her own web-based company rushed into her head, and she walked out into the sunshine in a daze. It wasn't going to happen. At least not this week. But maybe someday? Maybe Luke would miss her, maybe they could have a long-distance relationship. Maybe if she asked him to, he'd move to Seattle with her and the boys. Maybe someday all those impossible dreams could come true. Maybe if she stayed here, used her savings to get started, then things could develop with Luke at a natural pace. Too many maybes. She shouldn't drink wine during the day. It always gave her a headache.

She almost smacked herself. She had to get a grip. She wasn't even close to being as important to Luke as he had become to her. She'd had no indication that he would ever feel the same way she did. Indulgent, wishful, dangerous thinking. She needed to stop spinning dreams and face reality. She was in no position to turn down the best opportunity of her life to start her own business, and Luke was so tied to this town, it would take a miracle to make him leave.

****

"Mom, Mom, Mom!"

The boys ran into the house, Josh clutching an enormous turtle. "Look what we found."

Chloe wondered where Finn and Luke were, but she didn't ask. The children had probably worn the big boys out. She knew how easily that could happen. Add sun and water and turtles and, well, she wasn't surprised they'd dropped the boys off and rushed out of here.

"Should you have that in the house?" she asked. The poor turtle was out of its habitat. "Where'd you find it?"

"In the driveway! It would have got run over if Luke didn't stop the truck! We saved it! Can we keep it?"

"I don't think Dumpster would like that." Chloe noted the corner of the living room where Dumpster's cage had been set up when they arrived. The bunny munched on a large carrot and paid absolutely no attention to the turtle.

"He won't mind, will you, Dumpy?" Tommy said.

"Just like we don't mind going to live in Seattle,"

Josh said. His eyes were large and round and serious, his voice resigned.

Josh had been so upset when she'd first mentioned moving to Seattle. She'd hoped he'd gotten over that one brief burst of grief. Since then, neither boy had shown much interest in moving across the country. Nor did they complain about it.

"Grandma showed us where Seattle is on the atlas," Tommy said.

"It's really far," Josh said.

"Let's get this turtle back to his natural habitat before we talk about ours," Chloe said, leading the way firmly out the front door.

"Okay. Turtles. Do they like the water or the woods?" She kept one hand on each of her sons' shoulders.

"We could look it up online," Josh said. He wasn't letting go of the turtle.

"I'll do it," Tommy said. He went back into the house. He might be just six years old, but he knew the password to Chloe's laptop.

"Mommy, there's too many big words," Tommy said, bringing the laptop out to her.

They sat on the porch and watched the turtle as Josh finally set it down. It didn't move much.

"It says here that you should put it as close as possible to where you found it, but avoid roads. We're too close to the main road." Chloe read on.

"What kind of turtle is this guy?"

Josh came over and flicked through the DNR's pictures of Michigan turtles. "That's him." He pointed to a box turtle.

"Or her," Chloe said.

Both boys were highly insulted at the idea that "their" turtle could be a girl.

"Okay, so it says lakes and ponds."

"Mommy, that lake is too big. He needs to be able to live in some weeds." Josh pointed out another photo.

"Maybe Grandma knows where there's a pond around here. Or an inlet."

"What's an inlet?"

"It's like that place where we went swimming today."

"Oh," Tommy said.

"He doesn't like the cement," Josh said, moving himself and the turtle out to the grass.

Chloe closed her notebook and went out on the grass with the boys.

"Should we give him some water? He might be thirsty."

"Get a pail of water from the lake. I don't think we're supposed to give him anything not from his natural…"

"We know, Mom, his hab'tat."

Her phone rang. She pulled it out of her pocket and checked the screen. Luke.

"Hey," she said. She wondered if he'd got as much teasing about last night as she had endured. "Where can we find a pond or an inlet around here?"

He laughed. "Releasing the turtle back into the wild?"

"Yeah." Hearing his voice turned her bones soft. How could she leave when every inch of her being willed her to stay?

"Walk on the beach toward town. About halfway in there's a little stream that goes upriver."

"Thanks," she said. She wondered if he'd called for another reason. Or had he simply been doing due diligence on the turtle?

Chapter Thirteen

Luke left his house and went over to Main Street. Right behind the park, steps led to a public access walkway where people jogged or biked along the lake. He wished he had a dog, just for an excuse to be doing this. Or maybe he was past the point of needing excuses to see Chloe.

He wondered if Josh and Tommy would like a dog. He bet they'd love one.

After walking about ten minutes, he saw them up ahead, getting closer to the stream. Josh was probably carrying the turtle in the yellow pail he had in his hand, which was why Tommy kept peeking inside it.

Chloe looked effortlessly gorgeous, as usual. He wanted her with a strength that threatened to force him to break into a run to meet her. He wanted to grab her and hold her and kiss her. He wanted her and her boys in his life.

Luke kept his controlled amble until he got close enough to Chloe. "Just thought I'd make sure you found the stream okay."

Chloe blushed. Or maybe she had a little sunburn. The boys were all over him, insisting he show them exactly how far up the stream they should release the turtle, who they had named Ninja. The stream cut through town and turned into a river that ran several towns south and then back out to Lake Huron. People liked to take inner tubes and ride the river all day. A place on River Road rented those tubes. The boys would love it.

About to suggest they all go tubing tomorrow, what came out of his mouth instead, just after they let Ninja go into the sand next to some nice green scrub and with a perfect trickle of water leading up or down as the turtle wished to travel? An invitation to dinner in town.

"We're practically there," he said.

"Oh, I don't know," Chloe said.

"Mom! We're starving! Say yes."

"We've got a pizza parlor, a taco place, there's a guy who sells hot dogs from a cart in the park…"

"Hot dog!"

"Taco!"

"They make damn good margaritas," Luke said to Chloe, still dubious.

"I didn't bring my purse," she said.

"My treat. First we'll stop and get Tommy his hot dog, then we'll go to Sanchez's. We can sit on the patio and people watch. Come on. It will be fun."

"Come on, Mom. Pleeeease."

So Chloe let Luke take them to dinner. In order to get over her feelings that everyone in town watched them and might be taking mental notes for future gossip sessions, she drank her margarita (on the rocks, not frozen, yes, salt please) quickly. It settled her down somewhat, until her mother and Luke's mom strolled by with Luke's dad, who she'd never met.

"Well, look here, Wanda," Ursula said. "Isn't that your son, Daryl? 'Cause that's my daughter."

The trio stopped at the wrought iron railing that separated Sanchez's from the sidewalk traffic and called over the tables.

"Hi, Grandma!"

"We went fishing with Luke today."

Chloe ordered another margarita. A jumbo.

"You're not driving, I hope," her mother said.

"No. We walked down the beach."

Her mother moved toward the door of the restaurant, and Daryl and Wanda followed her. Soon, the three appeared on the patio while waiters hustled another table next to Luke and Chloe's.

"Honey, this is Daryl Anderson, Luke's daddy. And of course, you know Wanda."

"Nice to meet you," Chloe said to an older version of Luke.

They all sat down and took menus from the waiter. Another waiter brought Chloe's drink, just in time. She tried to sip it slowly, while Wanda introduced the boys to Daryl and Luke took a long pull of his beer.

"Luke helped us release a turtle back into the wild," Chloe said.

And then the boys had to tell the story of how Luke had rescued the turtle from the driveway and how they'd looked up what to do with him on the Internet.

"I did it," Tommy said.

"I had to read, though," Josh said.

"You are my best boys," Ursula said. Then she got tears in her eyes and batted them away but not before Chloe saw them. What was she doing? Why was she leaving her mother, the woman who had supported her and helped her build her life back up after she'd left Spence? This was the way she paid her mother back? By moving halfway across the country? Well, not halfway. All the way. To the very tip of the end of the line. As west as west could be.

She sighed and sipped her drink. Luke ordered another beer.

Tommy insisted he could still eat a taco even though he'd scarfed down a hot dog only minutes ago. And fries.

By the end of dinner, the boys were visibly wilting.

"Grandma, where's your car?"

"Just down the street, honey. Why? You want to ride back with me?"

Tommy clapped his hands. "Yes!" Josh, lost in thought, nodded agreement.

Chloe still had a good part of her jumbo margarita left, and Luke had half a beer, so her mother said, "You two stay and finish your drinks. I'll wait with the boys at the bungalow for you. I'll give them their baths."

Chloe did not have the heart to say no to her mother. This was the last week she'd be spending with her grandsons in a long time. She couldn't begrudge her mother time alone with them.

Before they left, Josh hugged Chloe and put his lips to her hair, muffling sound into her ears. "I wish we could stay here forever. I wish we didn't have to move to Seattle."

Chloe didn't think Luke heard what Josh said about Seattle. She hugged her boys and told her mom she'd be back at Blue Heaven soon. This was as good as a time as any to have the Seattle conversation with Luke. Everything depended on how he responded to the news.

Once they were alone, she looked around the patio. Nobody paid any attention to them. She lowered her voice anyway. "Everybody in town is talking about us. They know we spent the night together."

"Then let's go back to your place."

"Not with my boys—" Chloe's phone rang. Her mom.

"I just thought you'd let me have the boys stay at my place one more night," her mom said. Chloe heard the boys shouting "please" in the background.

"Okay." She was not about to begrudge her mom any time with the boys. Also, Luke sat across from her, begging her to take him home. "Let's go."

"Your mom? Got the kids?" Luke's slow, lazy smile rearranged his face from handsome to gorgeous.

"Yep." He thought this was Mom Plot stuff, but she knew better. Her mom wanted to give her time to tell Luke about Seattle.

****

"Take off your clothes." Luke's voice, muted by the shirt he pulled over his head.

All thought of Seattle flew from her head. He watched her, reaching out and pulling her close as she shed everything. No time to waste. Her vacation was running out. As the blues singer says, get it while you can.

But this time, Luke took charge, holding both of her hands above her as he licked and teased her breasts. When he gave one nipple a soft love bite, she said, "Harder." He granted her requests and let her arms go as he kissed his way down her belly.

He teased her inner thighs with long languid licks, first one side, then the other. Barely brushing her beach-ready lady parts. Then, all at once, he found her center and sucked until she moaned into her first orgasm of the evening.

After they'd used their mouths and tongues on each

Cynthia Harrison

other, after they made love twice before twilight fell, Seattle briefly asserted itself. She pushed her move to the far back of her love-saturated mind. She loved him. His tender kiss on her shoulder said he felt the same.

"God, I love you," he said, as if reading her thoughts.

She savored the words. "Ummm. Me too. Love you." She wasn't quite coherent, but that wasn't a crime under the influence of love in every sense of the word. In his strong arms, the salty scent of their love spilling onto the sheets, her eyes half-open gazing at his muscular pecs. Landscaping had an added benefit—his beautifully sculpted body. Luke did an honest day's work and used the amazing muscles God had given him to do it.

She soft next to his hard body. Vulnerable in a good way. She trusted him. Or did she? Because if she really trusted him, she'd tell him about Seattle and they'd work on a plan for being together there. Blue Lake was great for summer tourists and retired people, but could she make a life here? There were no businesses in need of her skills. Well, maybe small businesses, but she'd been working with a larger canvas. What was the school system like?

Stop it, she commanded herself. She'd worked too hard and too long for the top prize of an executive salary that would set her boys up for life. The job had fallen into her lap. Fate. Wasn't it?

By the time they'd showered and dressed, the night stars had turned on, reflecting off the placid water. Such a pretty piece of the planet. And so peaceful.

"Want to take a walk on the beach?"

"Yes." The moon came out to mellow her mood.

148

Maybe she'd have the courage to bring up the subject she most needed to talk to him about.

Chapter Fourteen

"You have to call her." Bettina sat in the only chair
the baby inside her liked these days, his recliner. Her
tummy so taut sometimes he saw a little foot kick out.
He knew what he had to do. He had to stop Chloe from
taking the boys away. Simple. Impossible.

"Calling won't cut it." Empowered, he knew the
actions he must take. He'd been networking online,
reaching out to old connections, reapplying for his
Realtor's license.

During a day of clicking from one link to another,
he found a vacant storefront in Blue Lake. In bold
lettering, the window said Blue Lake Real Estate. He
clicked around and found the backstory of how the
previous Realtor, who also handled summer rentals,
was on a very long vacation at a place she was unlikely
ever to leave, and a retired agent held down the fort.
The price tag so inexpensive, like the price of a
midsized car. Everything felt right. Why else would this
fall into his hands? Ursula was there for good now.
He'd spent many summers there with Chloe and the
boys. It seemed like a fine place to raise children. He
could tell Chloe that. The thought of confronting his ex
gave him the strong desire for a nice cold beer.

"Well, then, what will?" Bettina cut into his
thoughts.

"We're going up to Blue Lake. I'm going to tell her

I'll give her blood money back. I'll give her the house—"

Bettina drew in a sharp breath. They'd already decorated a nursery.

"Now, honey, wait a minute. I've been thinking, too. What do we need this mansion for? Housing prices are going up again, and mortgage rates are super low. I can sell this place myself, give Chloe half—would that be enough?"

"Should be." Days ago, he'd pulled comparable home prices. "I don't think we'll have a problem selling for a good price. People are having bidding wars."

"Good."

"Are you sure? What about the nursery?"

"We'll get a smaller place. We'll decorate a new nursery."

He was so thankful for his forgiving wife. She lost her bitterness the minute he got clean, and he saw pride shine from her eyes the minute he'd jumped back into real estate. Also probably relief. He'd been eating right and working out. He felt like he could do anything. After the all-too-brief moment of euphoric optimism, his mood swung back to negative. Chloe had his legal promise, written in blood.

"What?" Bettina could see the wheels in his head turning.

"Take six months maternity leave. If I can't support us, you can go back. But I will! I can do this."

"Having a job might keep you out of trouble." Bettina grinned in a wicked way extremely pregnant women really shouldn't. He wanted her.

"Can we still make love?" He wrapped his arms around her, kissing her hair. It smelled like flowers.

"I thought you'd never ask! Yes, we're still good, but not for long."

"We can always do other things." Spence was back. His libido had not been this strong in years. They made love, and he cuddled her the way he knew she liked while he talked about possible plans to pay his bitch ex-wife back. Have more contact with his kids, no matter how much it hurt when he had to let them go, over and over. All of them together in a small town like Blue Lake would be ideal.

"Did you mean it?" she asked. "You're going to Blue Lake?"

"We're going to Blue Lake. There's been a last minute cancellation on one of the cottages where Chloe and the boys are staying. You deserve a real vacation."

****

Chloe couldn't get the words out on the beach walk, with Luke holding her hand and the waves softly rolling in. She needed liquid courage before she confessed her Seattle secret.

She eyed the surroundings. There were the steps up to the town just ahead. Sanchez's, half a block away. And she was thirsty. As well as scared.

"I have to tell you something," she said.

Luke swung her hand in his as if the world was theirs for the taking.

"What?" He let go of her hand and took both her arms into his hands. His dear workingman hands. How she loved him. Every inch of him.

"It's not terrible, well, the thing is, do you mind?" She was not making sense out here in the wild night air with the wind whipping her hair. "Could we talk in Sanchez's? I'd love one more margarita."

"Sure," he said, taking her hand again and walking with her toward the beach steps.

"Second time tonight, Mr. Luke," said the hostess. Her bright Mexican costume showed all her assets, especially her cleavage, to great advantage. She was Luke's age but called him "mister" with a twinkle in her eye. She didn't give Chloe a glance as she led them to a secluded booth in back.

Luke sat next to her. He put his arm around her, and she leaned into him. She wanted always to be able to lean into this kind and sensitive man. He didn't ask what they needed to talk about, just sat with his arm around her while the waiter set down their drinks. A beer for him, a margarita for her.

Chloe had just taken the first lick of salt from the rim of her margarita when she heard a familiar voice.

"Hello, Chloe."

Spence. She spun in her seat. Bettina stood there, too. Spence held out his hand to Luke. "I'm Chloe's ex. This is my wife, Bettina."

They slid into the empty side of the booth.

Spence sat there like a rock of a guy. Sober and stubborn. Bettina's expression mirrored her husband's. Chloe did not have a good feeling about this at all.

"Spence, what are you doing here?" She looked at Bettina, who had always been her connection with the kids. They'd talked so often about Spence's addictions. So why did Bettina's eyes stab Chloe? Why was her mouth a bitter line? "Bettina?"

Hugely pregnant, Bettina seemed healthy, just tense. So nothing wrong with the baby. This had to be about…no, it couldn't be about the boys.

"Where are our sons?"

"Spending the night with my mom."

"One last night with grandma before the big move to Seattle?"

Chloe's heart dropped at the same time Luke dropped his arm from around her. He inched away from her. He didn't say hello to Bettina or shake hands with Spence. He didn't bother lowering his voice. He turned his head away from her.

"You're moving to Seattle? When were you planning on telling me? Or were you going to just leave without saying a word?"

Chloe froze. She could feel Luke's rejection in the physical space he created between them, in the way he said the words. She knew without looking that now, despite their "private" booth, the four of them had everyone's attention. Luke's cheeks were stained with a dark blush, so she knew he realized this, too.

When their waiter came and asked if Bettina and Spence wanted anything to drink, Spence stole a quick glance at Luke's beer, almost empty, then asked for coffee. Bettina shook her head no. "Another one, Mr. Luke?"

Chloe sucked her drink down so fast she got a headache. Spence's eyes widened. She wanted to make a nasty crack about his latest recovery efforts, but that wouldn't be nice.

"Just the check," Luke said.

Chloe finished her drink and pushed it to the side. She put her hands on her throbbed head. "That's what I was going to tell you," she said quietly.

Luke pulled several bills from his wallet, threw them on the table, and got up to leave. Chloe followed him outside, Spence and Bettina trailing after them.

"Could we go back down to the beach? Or somewhere more private?" She walked fast to keep up with Luke. He strode purposefully to his truck, parked, she saw, in the city lot next to the beach stairs. He must have driven it here when they met at the river to release the turtle. It seemed a million years ago.

"Get in." His voice terse, he didn't bother coming around to open her door as he usually did. "I'll drive you back to Blue Heaven."

Spence and Bettina caught up with them. "We're staying in Kiwi Cottage, so we'll talk more there," Spence said.

Great, Chloe thought. Just what she needed right before rolling out of town.

She got in the car. Her hands were cold although the night, even at this late hour, was warm.

As soon as they were inside the cocoon of the truck cab, Luke started the ignition and pulled out into the road with an excessive amount of tire screeching.

"I was going to tell you."

Luke's hands gripped the wheel so tight his knuckles were white. He sped down the road way too fast. He didn't say a word.

He braked hard in front of Blue Heaven. He didn't even bother pulling in off the road. The bonfire had started. People were out with their bags of marshmallows.

"Please. You have to let me explain."

He took his foot off the brake, stepped on the gas, and turned hard into the state park next to Blue Heaven.

"So explain," he said, throwing the car into park and cutting the motor.

Relief swept through like a broom. He would

listen. They could work things out. It would not be easy, but they could do it. She had faith in them. Spence showing up was a speed bump. Chloe did not want to talk about Spence. She wanted to erase him.

Luke could hardly hear Chloe's words above the roar in his own head.

"Before I met you, it seemed sheer good luck to get this offer," she said. "It's a lot of money. My ex is an addict. He has never paid a dime of child support. I paid off his house for him. His wife works. He stays home and gets high."

"He ordered coffee."

"Yeah, well, he's been to rehab a number of times. Things were getting bad back in Sterling Pines. Bettina and I talked about his escalation. Even the kids mentioned to me that they'd found him passed out with a liquor bottle the last time they stayed with him."

"Well. Maybe the thought of his children moving across the country caused him to take desperate measures." The bottom had dropped out of Luke's world, like his first pickup in high school, when the undercarriage began to rust away and he had to watch where he put his feet.

"Dude seemed sober tonight. Maybe he's straightened up for good this time. It happens. I've seen it. Eddie, the guy who owns the bar? He was a drunk for twenty years. He tried to quit twenty times. Now he owns a bar and hasn't had a drink in five years."

Luke steamed at the thought of Chloe doing the same thing to him that Amber had done when she'd taken Bella away. "I see he's got another one coming. How can you take your kids away from their father? Their new sibling? Your mom?" Luke didn't speak his real thoughts: *How can you take them from me? How can you leave me?*

Chloe told him another story, this one about how easily and painlessly Spence had signed the paperwork allowing her to leave the state with the boys once he realized he'd be off the hook forever with child support. She had a pocketful of excuses, but none of them cut it with him.

"But what about the boys? Don't you care that they need their father?" He had wanted to be their father, he only now realized. It wasn't Spence he meant, it was him. Not good to take them from Spence, no matter what sort of fuck up the man had been, but what really hurt, what he could not stand, was her taking them from him before he even got a chance to be a dad to them.

He hadn't been staring at her, but now with the moon out from behind the pines, he stole a glance and saw the guilt on Chloe's face.

"I do feel bad about that," she said. "But I'm the parent. The only parent right now who's looking out for them. I have to decide what's best. And bottom line, we need money to live, and I have to earn it." When she mentioned her salary, he felt a little sick. He might see that kind of money in three or four good years. "I want my kids to have a good life. I want them to go to college."

Luke tried to move his eyes away, but the way her hair shone in the moonlight made it impossible. Her scent: moonlight and roses. But she had a coldness in her. To do this to her boys, she must. "So it hurt when Spence walked out on your marriage. He may be a jerk, but he doesn't deserve to lose contact with his children."

Chloe stared down at her hands in her lap. "Who told you Spence left me?"

"Nobody. I—didn't he?"

"I left him."

"Why?"

Chloe had been through this with friends when the breakup had happened. So many times, she'd memorized the words. "I don't think he'll ever get sober. Not for good. I think he'll struggle the rest of his life. I don't want us to be part of that struggle."

Luke could understand that. But still. She didn't have to stay married to the guy. And if they lived here, there would be plenty of supervised visitation. He believed that a split family could mend itself with love. He'd seen it happen with friends. Blue Lake was a small town. People had roots here, and they didn't leave when they busted up. They stayed and formed a new kind of family. Well, Amber didn't do that, but most people from around here, the ones who stayed, did just fine.

"And here he is. Breaking us up. I know the signs. Fresh out of rehab. Again." She started to cry, very softly. He steeled himself not to touch her. She talked on and on about how Spence had not abused her. He had not beaten her, not physically anyway. He had been a drug addict and an alcoholic. Emotionally absent. Checked out. He hadn't cheated on her. He had been a good provider, once upon a time. Her reason for leaving hadn't been anything he'd done to her, but more the things he'd neglected to do for her and the kids. Like love them. Respect her. Treat her with kindness. Stay sober for all of them.

Luke didn't know how to reply. He shifted in his

seat and spun the inert wheel. Her words sounded full of pain, and her reasons were sound. How to tell her that half-formed plan in his head, the plan he didn't let himself think about very often, the plan that moved more than one date at a time, which is how he'd been trying to take his relationship with Chloe? Despite his rule, already broken and tossed away, he'd moved ten steps ahead on the chessboard in his head. He thought she had, too. They loved each other. They were in this thing together. So were the boys. The only thing left to do was settle the details. Or so he'd thought.

"You know that day when Spence dropped off the boys and you were the only person home?" Her voice dragged him back to the reality of the situation now. Not as he'd hoped it would eventually, all in good time, become. He nodded.

"That's Spence. He doesn't think beyond his own needs. He never put the boys before what he wanted, and he never put me first, ever." Chloe raked her fingers through her hair, pulling it away from her face. Now the moon played on her cheekbone. She had exquisite skin. He hated her. He loved her. Hated what she'd done. Blaming Spence and not mentioning them, what they had. Or what they'd started.

He watched her lower her eyes, concentrating on what story to tell next. He didn't want to hear anything else. He just wanted to leave it, leave them all to sort out their own mess. But somehow, without him wanting it, the thing had become his mess too. He was part of it now. And she deserved to be heard out.

"When I was in labor with Tommy…" She kept her eyes down.

This story was a hard one for her. For one thing,

she practically whispered. Longing and hopelessness filled every silence between her halting words. She stopped, and when it seemed she wouldn't, or couldn't, go on, she blurted, "You could come with us." Their eyes aligned, hers widened in shock by what she'd said.

Hell, maybe she'd been thinking ahead, too. A different game than his. Moves he would not dream of making. He let a whoosh of breath out through his nose. "I would never leave my folks. I'm their only child. My work is here. This is my home, Chloe." He'd had it. He had to leave her now, or she'd be moving him into her Seattle mansion as his pool boy. He turned the key, to start the truck. Her signal to move on. Move up in the world. Away from here and their simple way of living.

Words tumbled from her mouth. Where she'd been slow, now she tripped over them. "My pains came on super strong, right away. I knew something wasn't right. It wasn't that way with Josh. I timed them and they were only a few minutes apart. I called Spence around five o'clock in the morning. Still out partying. Spence finally answered after the third call to his cell. He said to have my mom take me to the hospital and watch Josh."

Luke kept the motor running, pulled the shoulder closest to her away and up. Was she blaming Spence for the break-up of the marriage? Hadn't it been her decision? Didn't they have marriage counselors downstate? Everyone knew it took two people to make a marriage and two people to split it up.

"Spence said he'd be there when he could. He missed the birth. He missed the first day of Tommy's life. He came into the hospital at regular visiting hours that night, stinking of beer. And the first thing he said, before he even asked how I was, before he even saw the baby, was that he'd had a hell of a day and he hoped I wasn't about to bust his balls."

Okay. Horrible story and despite his determination to break things off now, while it could still be done relatively painlessly, he imagined how it must have been for her. "What did he say when you told him you wanted a divorce?"

"At first, we tried counseling. I thought that by the end of therapy, I'd be able to somehow solve my problem, live with an addict. He went to one session and then said I had the problem so I should be the one to go to a shrink. It turned out that I did have a problem. A big one named Spence."

She'd stopped loving him. Luke would not say this, but the thought came through despite his best intentions to leave her and her long sad story alone.

"I didn't love him anymore. He'd killed that with his drinking and drugging. He got fired from his job a month before he told me. We almost lost our house. My mom had to bail us out. He'd had addiction problems in the past, but he'd been to rehab and supposedly fixed. Again. Except he wasn't. One day Tommy came out of Spence's office with a vial of white powder clutched in his little hand. That was it. The end. I took my kids to my mom's that day and never looked back."

"So the guy had to work hard. So he sometimes had a bad day. Addicts relapse all the time. But then they get clean again. And their family stands beside them. Life is not all hearts and flowers and romance." Luke purposely came up with every reason not to love her, not to beg her to stay. He'd been a dumb ass and broken his rule, and now he was paying the price. He needed it to stop now.

"My therapist said Spence was an emotional abuser."

He wanted to say he was sorry she'd chosen the wrong man. But "Have a good life" came out instead. He reached over across her lap and opened the passenger door. He gunned the engine for good measure.

She sat there, taking no hints. "So this is it? We're over? You won't even consider my offer? You said you loved me. I love you. That's the important part. That's what matters."

"I told you why I won't move." He had to get her out of his truck, and then he had to go home and have a beer in his empty living room. "We should have never happened. Would have never happened had I known you were moving to Seattle. When? Tomorrow? The next day?" He didn't have to fake the venom in his voice. He wanted to hit something. Maybe that wall in his kitchen that needed taking down anyway.

He didn't look when he heard her scoot off the seat and lower herself to the ground. With most of his mind, he thought about where he'd last seen his crowbar. A tiny part watched her walk past the stand of pines over to Blue Heaven before he backed out of the lot and headed back into town. Home.

Chapter Fifteen

Chloe carefully wove through the stand of pines that divided the park from Blue Heaven. Luke hadn't even mentioned love. Not once. When she got to the bonfire, the kids were with Spence and Bettina. Her mom must have let Spence take them. They were so happy to see their dad. Chloe's heart broke for the second time in ten minutes. Her smile wobbled as she called for bedtime.

"The sofa in Kiwi cottage turns into a bed! Daddy says we can sleep on it." The words toppled out of Josh.

"Please," Tommy begged.

"Only if your mom says it's okay." Bettina, always the voice of reason and the only reason Chloe said yes. It gave her an excuse to go into her room right now and be alone with her misery.

She kissed her boys goodnight and headed for her room in the bungalow, but sleep didn't come easy that night. She grabbed a few fitful hours, then gave in and got up. She put a pot of coffee on the stove and went out to the porch to watch the sun come up.

Spence wandered out of Kiwi early. He carried his own mug of coffee and sat down uninvited in the deck chair next to hers. They didn't speak, as if neither was willing to start. Finally, Spence began his familiar tale: he'd stay clean and sober this time, he had returned to work, he would pay her back, turn his life around, blah,

163

blah, blah.

Chloe tuned out briefly, until he began to talk about moving to Blue Lake. "I put our house on the market yesterday, and it sold to the first guy who walked through the door this morning."

She sat up straighter and peered into her coffee mug. Empty. She still didn't feel like talking, so she held up her index finger and gestured with her coffee cup.

Spence followed her into the kitchen. "This is nice. We'd like something along these lines up here. Obviously, not on the lake. Out of our price range."

"So glad I could help you get your future together." She couldn't resist the dig, him basically using her money to create a new life.

Spence went on as if he had not heard her.

"Did you know there's an empty real estate office right next to Sanchez's? It seems too good to be true." He held out his cup and she filled it. "This could work for all of us, Chloe."

"I already have a plan. A plan that does not include living in Michigan. You signed off on me taking the kids out of state."

"I know." They stood, not really looking at each other, unwilling to share the small table that had a window out to the lake. "I was wrong. I should not have done that. As you know, under the influence at the time."

"We're leaving in a few days. There's nothing you can do about it."

"Well, there is, but let's not fight. Can't you see? This place is perfect for starting over. Housing, especially those old cottages like your mom's that aren't on the lake, is super cheap here. People are buying again. When our house sold, I realized there's a housing shortage and a historic low on mortgage rates."

"But, Spence, what about Bettina's career?"

"What about it? She wants to stay home with the baby."

Of course she did. Chloe thought with a twinge about how lovely it had been this past month being there for her boys every day. Not having to rush off to work or chain herself to her laptop on weekends. All that was about to change. Spence talked on.

"People start over every day. I know I screwed up our marriage and wasn't there for you and the kids. But I've really learned my lesson. I can do it right this time."

How often had she heard that tune? A click alerted Chloe to Wanda's entry into the registration office. She checked the clock. Already eight. Wanda of course smelled the coffee and gave a quick knock.

"Come on in," Chloe said, wondering if Luke had told Wanda about Seattle and her domestic distress.

Another key turned in a lock, and Wanda stood in the kitchen, her mouth opening and closing when she noted Spence.

"Hi," Spence said, cheery as Chloe was glum.

"Kiwi? Right?"

"Yep."

"Where are the little ones, Chloe?"

"This is their dad. Spence, Wanda. Wanda, Spence. They spent the night in Kiwi."

Wanda stared hard at Chloe. That woman did not miss a trick. She must know some of what had gone on yesterday, if not all. Nobody knew Luke had broken up with her. Not yet. Spence's voice penetrated again.

"Love your town." He spoke to Wanda with enthusiasm she remembered from the young, sober Spence. "My wife and I, and our new baby, are moving here permanently. Trying to talk Chloe here out of going to Seattle with my boys. She should stay here, too. That's the proper way to blend a family."

Cripes. As if he knew the first thing about it. Wanda had yet to utter a word, her mouth opening again to form an O as her head swept from Chloe to Spence.

"Well," she finally said, "you're right about this town. It's a great place to raise kids. We look out for each other here."

Noise built from the cottagers who craved Wanda's freshly baked muffins. Wanda transferred the coffee Chloe had made into a large carafe, started a new pot, and went out to say hi and situate the coffee pot and muffins upstairs.

"See? Even she thinks it's a good idea."

"Spence." Bettina came in, a boy holding each of her hands.

"Hi, baby." He set down his cup and went over to hug his wife. The hug lasted a long time. The boys came to Chloe and began talking over each other about how cool it had been to stay in Kiwi cottage.

"When are we going to the beach?"

"Right now." Chloe figured the very pregnant Bettina would not follow them there. Plus they were house-hunting. And Spence had to check on his new office space.

Spence's cell phone rang. He answered and gave short answers. Chloe worried he'd get an injunction to keep her in state. He'd hinted at it, and she knew he could play dirty when he wanted to. God, she hated him.

Spence slipped his cell into his shorts pocket. "That was Ursula." His eyes shone with excitement. "She told me she put in a good word with the guy who owns the bank."

Why did he have to say that in front of the kids? Curious guests gathered at the pocket door, currently wide open, that separated living quarters from work space. Wanda bustled in and unplugged the larger pot to carry it upstairs. Spence insisted he carry it. Too heavy for her, he said. As if Wanda didn't do this very job every day. Bettina followed Spence out into the public area, and Wanda firmly locked the family space from prying eyes, several of which had been children the boys' ages.

"Okay," Chloe said. "Eat your cereal, and we'll go to the beach."

"Are you going to pack sandwiches and juice boxes?"

"Of course. But you still have to eat your cereal."

"You buy the most boringest cereal. Dad had chocolate cereal in his cottage."

Figures. The sober Spence had a serious sweet tooth.

The boys quickly shoveled down the boring cereal and went to put on their bathing suits. Wanda knocked and Chloe told her to come in.

She sat at the kitchen table while Chloe cleared the cereal bowls, still sloshing with milk.

****

Luke had escaped from Chloe and all her baggage

with his heart intact. He didn't give his love away easily, and now he knew for certain why he shouldn't break the only rule he had when he came to letting a woman into his life.

He'd done the day's work on autopilot, and his house was dark when he got there. Chloe had never seen it, a good thing. He turned on the hall light and looked around the empty spaces. This he knew. This he was used to. He went into his living room, turned on the ball game. This room had one chair, one table, and one television. It met his needs. Tigers were losing, batting zero to six in the last inning.

She's just like Abby. He went to the kitchen, opened the fridge, pulled out a beer. Why did he have to fall in love with her? Sure, it had been great hanging with her and the boys. But that wasn't love. He hadn't really known her then. Now he did.

The Tigers struck out, Don-O hit a pop up way out in the field, ending the inning and the game. He clicked off the television and sat drinking his beer. This gloomy and quiet house seemed unnatural after spending so much time with two talkative little boys. He might have misjudged Chloe, but her kids were all right. Hell, he had enjoyed the times he'd spent with them. Josh, always so serious, except when joy rose in his eyes and his little body hopped with excitement. Tommy, a bundle of live wires, always sparking off happy vibes. He'd miss them.

He finished his beer and took the bottle into the kitchen. He kept the empty case right next to the fridge. Not very stylish but convenient. Chloe would have tried to fix things up around here. Women were famous for that. He rinsed the bottle out at the sink before stacking it into the case.

The newspaper folded onto the sports section on the table where he'd left it this morning. He didn't want another beer. It would work with his mood to bring him down farther than he wanted to go. He sat to read the paper, but couldn't concentrate. He kept thinking about what Chloe had said. The whole "unfulfilled" woman bullshit. Any woman who would take her kids so far away from everyone who loved them and everything they knew, was not the kind of woman for him. Better to learn that now. End of story.

He pulled the sports section out of the paper and went back into the living room. He'd find another game somewhere on cable. But he clicked through the channels without seeing anything of interest. He'd thought for sure Chloe had been falling under the spell of Blue Lake. He'd seen it happen time after time. People came for vacation and then found a way to stay.

His heart hammered in his chest. She had asked him to move to Seattle with them. Had she meant it? It didn't matter. Any woman who would break up a home, deprive her children of a father for purely selfish reasons, not a woman for him. He resolutely put Chloe and her children out of his mind.

Chapter Sixteen

Two days went by, and Chloe didn't hear a word from Luke. Not that she expected to. Her mother didn't mention him, Eva didn't mention him, the boys didn't mention him more than a million times.

It was as if she'd made it all up. Or as if he was just another guy out for a good time, not thinking of what happens next but only what happens now.

The Seattle job waited. She really had no choice. She had to do the best thing she could for her kids. To stay here would just be to hope and hang around waiting for Luke to say he loved her. That would not happen.

She sat on the beach as the boys built castles in the sand. That's what dreaming of a life with Luke was like—a castle made of sand. When she got to Seattle, everything would be clear again. She'd be working like a machine again, she'd be in control, she'd have money and a house and a nanny for her boys. Her life would line itself right back up again.

That night, the boys begged to stay up late at the fire. Her mom showed up with a fresh bag of marshmallows. Spence and Bettina were there. Eva sat down next to Chloe when Tommy got up to run to his grandmother.

"How are you?" Eva asked.

"Fine." Chloe hoped Eva wouldn't bring up Luke.

She'd been thinking about what he'd said the past few days. Doubting herself. Was it wrong to take her kids away from their father? Their grandmother? "Where's Daniel tonight?"

She tried to distract herself by asking about Eva's husband. She'd have plenty of time for the boys. There would be nobody else, after all. Just work. And them. Every move she made was for them. So they'd have stability, insurance, a college fund.

"He's working on a project." Eva stopped speaking for a minute, touched Chloe's hand. "You've been so quiet the last couple of days."

Chloe nodded. "I'm okay. It's just—"

"What?"

"Luke and I had a fight."

Before she could say anything more, the boys crowded around her with their s'more sticks and freshly roasted marshmallows.

Eva got up so Tommy could have his seat back. "I won't see you tomorrow. Daniel and I are going to Traverse City for a long weekend. So have a safe trip. Email when you get to Seattle."

"I will," Chloe said. Then she finished making her boys their final s'mores.

The next day, Josh didn't want to collect treasure on the beach with Chloe and Tommy, so she let him stay in the bungalow for an hour with his handheld video game. Josh was a good kid, a responsible boy, and Wanda was on the property, taking care of the daily chores.

Tommy was such a happy child. Any little piece of smooth rock or glass thrilled him, and he reverently placed it into his yellow pail.

"Mommy?" Tommy had his head down, searching the sand.

He bent down to dig and then let the waves wash his latest find, a bottle cap. Just another treasure to Tommy.

"Why doesn't Josh want to move to Seattle?"

Chloe's skin turned to gooseflesh even though the sun beat down.

"Is it because it's so far away? From Daddy? I'll miss my daddy too, but he can come on weekends, right? And Grandma. We can still spend the night with her sometimes, right? Josh says we can't. He says it's too far. But it's not too far, right, Mommy? Right?"

Chloe took Tommy's hand and led him over to the shore, away from the water. They sat down together.

"It actually is a little too far, honey. Josh is right."

Tommy's hurt expression was like she'd slapped him.

"But Mommy, I'm going to have a new brother. Or it might be a sister, it's a surprise. But I have to be the big brother now. And big brothers have to be there. You know that!"

Chloe sighed.

"Let's go see how Josh is doing, and then we can all talk about this together."

Tommy still seemed upset, but he followed Chloe when she got up and led the way toward the bungalow.

Back at the house, no sign on Josh. Chloe noticed that Dumpster, cage and all, was also missing. Oh-oh.

"Wanda, have you seen Josh?" Chloe found Wanda in the laundry room, folding sheets.

"He said he was taking that rabbit for a walk," Wanda said. "I just figured you'd meet him on the beach."

There had been an old red wagon out by the shed. Eva said it was from when she'd been a girl, and she allowed the boys to play with it. Now Chloe couldn't find the wagon. It wasn't Wanda's fault. She was working, not babysitting. But now Chloe felt real fear, dark and chilling. Josh would not take the wagon and the rabbit, in his cage, down to the beach. There were too many steps. He must have gone down the highway.

She quickly checked Josh's room. His backpack was gone and his toys and clothes were strewn around the room.

"Come on, Tommy, we need to find Josh."

"Oh, dear," Wanda said. "I'm sorry, honey."

"It's not your fault," Chloe said. "I'm sure he's fine."

Chloe's call to her mother's cell went to voice mail. She and Tommy had been at the beach less than a half hour. Josh couldn't have gone far. But what if someone had picked him up off the road?

Her heart beat wildly. Her stomach sickened. Tommy picked up on Chloe's distress and started crying.

Chloe knew she'd go out of her mind in another minute if she didn't take action.

"Wanda, if Josh comes back, would you please call me?"

She wrote her number down on a pad in the kitchen with shaky hands.

She might throw up, but she had to go right now. She had to find Josh.

"Come on, Tommy." She grabbed keys from her bedroom.

She couldn't move fast enough, and yet time crawled by. Once she had Tommy safely belted into the car, she pulled out onto the road, hyper-conscious of the speeding traffic. Blue Heaven was on the main road into town, the main road for the entire thumb of Michigan. Lower speed limits were posted in Blue Lake, but people often blew by them going twice the legal limit. Only a thin shoulder off the road. Josh could have been hit, could be bleeding by the roadside, hit by a crazy summer driver.

Her phone rang on the console and without taking her eyes off the road, clicked on speaker and said, "Yeah?"

"Josh is pulling a red wagon with Tommy's rabbit in it down Strobell Avenue," Luke said. "The rabbit's in a cage."

"You see him? You have your eyes on him right now?"

"Yes."

Chloe let out a breath she hadn't known she'd been holding.

"Okay. Please don't let him out of your sight. I'm downtown, near the beach steps. How do I get to Strobell?"

"Go down two streets to Taylor. Take a left. I'll stay on the line until you find us."

"Is that where your house is?"

"No, I'm doing lawns."

"Okay. Turning left on Taylor." Her knees were weak. Now was not the time to think of what might have happened. She sent a thousand thank-yous heavenward.

"Keep on Taylor. Strobell is down three or four

blocks. Turn right. It's a long street. He hasn't even seen me yet, but I recognized his shirt and ball cap."

"I'm on Strobell. Oh, I see him." She clicked off the phone without saying good-bye. Josh, small and defenseless in his orange Tiger T-shirt. His little shoulder blades were hunched, and he trudged along like the weight of the world rested on his small back. Chloe drove slowly by him, but he didn't notice. She pulled into the driveway, which was when she noticed Luke had put away his riding lawnmower and only pretended to sweep the cut grass off the sidewalk. He had both eyes on her boy. This broke her heart, but she pushed that particular misery aside. Luke didn't know her at all.

She put the car in park, effectively blocking Joshua, who stopped his progress, red wagon and all. Anguish stood clear on his face.

He usually kept his expressions tucked away inside, and Chloe could see him fold up his disappointment and sadness. He looked at her, gauging her reaction.

She ran over and hugged him, lifting him off the ground. Gratitude for his safety flooded her; she whispered a brief prayer of thanks to the sky.

"Where were you going, honey?"

"To Grandma's." He squirmed in her arms, as he did these days after hugs longer than a few seconds in duration.

Chloe glanced around in a daze. Her mother *did* live somewhere around here. Next block? She wasn't sure.

"I used the GPS on your iPhone," he said. "Up at that next street, you turn right, and that's Grandma's street."

She hadn't known her iPhone had a GPS. Or that Josh knew how to download apps, which required her password, another thing she had not even imagined he knew.

"Well, I'll take you the rest of the way there," she said. She opened the back door for Josh to climb in, noticing that Luke rested an arm on the open window on Tommy's side of the car, talking to him. While Josh got in the car, she put Dumpster, cage and all, in the front seat next to her. Luke hoisted the red wagon into the trunk. Josh's backpack, stuffed with every item of clothing he'd brought with him on vacation, sat on the sidewalk where Chloe and Luke both reached for it. Chloe tried hard to hold in the tears.

"Just give it to Josh," she said, and got into the driver's seat, blinking her eyes. "And, Luke, thank you."

"No problem," Luke said, as she backed out of the driveway and headed for her mother's house.

He waved as they passed, but only Tommy waved back.

"He told you where I was, didn't he?"

Chloe's upset body didn't trust her voice to speak. Upset began turning into anger. She needed a calm place where she could talk to Josh like the adult he needed her to be right now. So she just nodded and kept driving.

"Mommy was so worried about you," Tommy said. "But I wasn't."

Josh made some reply. Chloe's ears roared, waves of anger and helplessness threatened to overtake her. She wondered if she should go back to the bungalow and handle this alone. But there would be more people there, all the folks who'd rented cottages, their kids, Wanda, feeling responsible, even though she wasn't. Worst of all, Spence and Bettina. Oh, they'd love to get in the middle of this.

So she drove to her mother's. There were several cars in the driveway. Oh great. Mah-jongg at Mom's. Chloe called her mom from the car.

"We have a situation here."

"Did you find him? Wanda called me. She's beside herself."

"Yes, we're in your driveway."

"That's fine, honey, the girls were just leaving." Chloe figured she'd probably broken up the game, but relief tempered anxiety when women began to appear on the porch and walk down the steps of her mother's cute little cottage. They waved to her and the boys and got into their cars and drove off.

Tommy was already out and like a shot up the porch and into his grandmother's house. Josh hung back to take care of Dumpster. It tore Chloe's heart out to see such a little boy handle the awkward wire cage. But Josh took the cage by both arms and walked with Dumpster into his grandmother's house. Chloe brought up the rear.

She knew, as soon as she got inside, that the game had not been over. A full plate of sandwiches graced the kitchen table, and an uncut cake sat on the counter. Dishes of peanuts and Chex mix dotted the card tables, one still set up with a mah-jongg game, all the tiles spread on the table in front of the chairs.

"Can we play, Grandma?" Tommy said, sitting right down and picking up the intricately designed tiles.

"Sure, honey," Ursula said.

"Josh, I hear you were coming over to visit me."

"Yeah. Mom"—he looked at her—"I'm sorry, but I can't go to Seattle with you. It's too far. You can take Tommy, but I have to stay here with Grandma. And Dad. They need us, too."

Chloe's anger at Josh drained away in an instant, replaced by a heavy sense of profound sadness. She had done this. She had made her child choose between his parents. Her self-hatred raged, out of control.

"I looked up Seattle on the Internet, and Mom, it's 3,272 miles away. It takes more than a whole day to get there if you drive without stopping even to pee. Almost two days. But it would be more, because you'd have to stop to eat and go to the bathroom."

"I know, honey, but there are airplanes. You can fly in to see your dad, and Grandma already said she'd come see us this winter."

Josh shook his head.

"I'm sorry, Mom. I really am. But I thought about it and I can't do it. Dad needs us, too."

A wave of nausea rolled through Chloe.

"Did you talk to Dad?"

Josh nodded.

"He doesn't want us to leave. He said I couldn't live with him and Bettina and the baby, so I thought Grandma might have room for me."

"Of course I have room for you!" Ursula said, bending down to fold Josh into her arms. Traitor, Chloe thought.

"Mom!" Chloe's voice was sharper than she'd intended. "Josh is my child. I have sole custody of him. He doesn't get to decide where he lives. He lives with me. That's it."

Josh turned out of his grandmother's arms and flew into her spare bedroom, the one she'd already fixed up for the two boys. He slammed the door.

Chapter Seventeen

Ursula eyed Chloe, who held her mother's gaze. Tommy came into the kitchen and nabbed a sandwich from the plate on the table.

"Mom. Listen. You are not helping," Chloe said.

"Then why are you here? Why didn't you just go home and handle this yourself? Oh, that's right. You don't have a home. I'm sorry, Tommy." Ursula looked at the little boy. "Take a sandwich in to Josh, would you?"

"We can eat in the bedroom?"

"Just this once."

Tommy went to the pantry and pulled out two juice boxes. Then he put them down and went over to Dumpster's cage, where he removed the empty water dish and filled it. He gave Dumpster his water and a carrot from the fridge, and then he picked up the juice boxes and sandwiches and went into the bedroom with his brother.

Chloe tried to speak, but her voice choked with tears. Her mother, the one person she could always count on to be on her side, had betrayed her.

"I'm sorry, dear, but this is, well, it's not how I planned on things working out."

"Please don't tell me you planned for me and Luke to get married and live happily ever after."

Ursula actually laughed.

"Well, Wanda and I did entertain some hopes in that direction, but now I see it's not in the cards."

That stung. Chloe was the one in love. She was the one being rejected. By Luke, and now by her own son. Suddenly her knees couldn't hold her up any more. She fell hard into a kitchen chair, pushed the plate of sandwiches away, and put her head down on the cool Formica tabletop.

"You're right. Josh is your boy. Of course I shouldn't have said that. But he broke my heart."

Chloe lifted her head like her neck had a heavy bag of sand on it.

"I knew he felt sad about this. And I could kill Spence." Chloe lowered her voice. "You heard that part about how Josh couldn't live with him. What kind of parent doesn't say an open-hearted yes to his own child when that child asks to be taken in?"

"Spence has always been about Spence. You know that. And his wife is pregnant. She'd not going to want to be dealing with an eight-year-old." Ursula whispered too. The last thing they wanted was for Josh to hear them.

Chloe's stomach churned as if she were in a boat atop choppy water. She wasn't sure of anything anymore except that her new job waited, and it would change all of their lives for the better. Eventually.

She dug in her purse for a Rolaid. She kept them in there since the days of her high-stress ex-job, when she'd popped them with regularity. She hadn't needed one since the day she'd quit. Soon, she'd be in an even higher stakes situation. She'd be playing with the big boys. Seattle. Shit. She could handle it, of course she could. Completely up to the challenge. But would her family survive?

The boys came out of the bedroom and turned on the television. Tommy brought the empty juice boxes into the kitchen.

"Mom, is it true Josh gets to stay here with Grandma and I have to go all the way to the other end of the country?" His eyes glossed with unshed tears. The minute he finished his sentence, the tears fell and he started to wail. Chloe took him up in her lap and let him cry into her shoulder, soaking her t-shirt.

"No, baby, that's not true. Josh is leaving with us. We're all going together. The three of us are a team."

Tommy hiccupped in his last cries.

"You promise?"

"I do."

If Josh heard what she said from the living room, he didn't indicate it. He kept his eyes on the television, which played an infomercial for a blender that could grind potatoes into liquid in thirty seconds.

"Grandma, can we watch *Shrek*?"

"Sure, kiddo. You know how to work that machine better than I do."

Tears forgotten, Tommy ran back into the living room. The house was so small that Chloe could almost reach out and touch her boys if she needed to. She needed them that close. Even closer. She glanced with longing at the sofa. The boys sat on the floor in front of the television, sprawled on the huge pillows her mother kept just for them. They had positioned themselves under the card tables as if they were in bunkers.

"Go ahead."

Her mom knew what Chloe needed. She always knew.

Chloe went and sat on the sofa to watch *Shrek* for the tenth or twentieth time. Nobody spoke. A truce, for the time being, had been called.

She fell asleep in the middle of the movie. She woke with a start as the credits rolled on the screen and the boys got up from their prone positions to stretch.

"What are we gonna do now?"

"Now," her mom said, coming into the living room, which had been cleared of the card tables and mah-jongg tiles. "We're going to get that sprinkler going out back. Anybody want to put on his bathing suit?"

"Yay!" Tommy said. Josh followed him into the bedroom to change.

"I know Josh brought some clothes, but Tommy doesn't have a suit here," Chloe said.

"Of course he does, dear. I bought him one. Plus pajamas and blue jeans and T-shirts and underwear. What else would I keep in their dresser drawers?"

Chloe looked at her mother like she'd never met the woman before. When her mother had left Sterling Pines and moved up north, some small corner of her heart had been abandoned. It was the right thing to do for all of them, and it wasn't a fair comparison, but she understood at last Spence's sadness at being orphaned. Now she saw that her mother had never intended to cut them loose at all. She knew Chloe could stand on her own, start a life, soar.

And that's what Chloe had tried to do, what she could do successfully and securely, with the job in Seattle.

"Mom. This is so hard."

"I know, dear, but you'll work it out. You always

do. Now here's a list. I want to make the boys meatloaf for dinner."

Her mother handed Chloe a list and opened the wallet she held in her other hand.

"No, Mom, I'll buy the food if you cook," Chloe said. The boys came out in their bathing suits.

"I'll be right back. Going to the store for Grandma." She could tell by the smug grin on Josh's face that he thought he'd won. He thought he'd turned back the clock and that they'd all stay here with her mother in Blue Lake in this little cottage. Was not going to happen. But she couldn't deal with telling him that right now.

Right now, all she could do was drive to the grocery store.

Inside the over air-conditioned town grocery store, numb with cold, her mind worked. Her son, her beloved boy, had chosen to live with his father. And this broke her heart more than the other part, Spence had refused.

She trudged through the store, list in hand, her heart ripped from her body. The produce section, one skinny aisle of withered fruit and vegetables left over from the weekend Farmer's Market, beckoned. Most people bought from their neighbor's farm stands, but luckily she only needed onions and potatoes.

She wanted to call Spence and yell at him. The idiot could have said yes to their boy, to spare him hurt, and then she could have been the mean mom and refused. Spence *knew* she'd refuse. How could he have been so thoughtless?

She aimed her cart at the meat counter, asking the butcher for two pounds of ground beef. How was she going to fix this?

She was used to the grocery store back home. She'd have to get used to a new grocery store in Seattle. Well, maybe the nanny would be doing the shopping. She'd have to work that out. Right at this minute, she hated shopping for food. It seemed pointless because she'd never be able to eat again. But the boys needed to be fed. So she walked up and down the unfamiliar aisles, all eight of them, sightless. It took her three slow trips to find ketchup and bread crumbs and Jell-O.

She paid for the food on auto-pilot. Drove back to her mother's. She didn't see Luke on Strobell or any other street.

The boys were playing a video game.

"You forgot the eggs, Chloe!"

Her mother sounded exasperated but sympathetic.

"Oh."

"Never mind. Run up again while I peel these potatoes."

Her body dragged, heavy like the ten pound sack of potatoes sitting on the kitchen counter. But she put one foot in front of the other and did what her mother told her to do. When she got back to the cottage again, the boys were still playing video games, the potatoes were bubbling in a pot of water on the stove, and the meatloaf mixture minus eggs sat in a blue bowl. Her mom had used that same mixing bowl since Chloe was a little girl.

Her mother broke three eggs into the bowl and dug her hands into the ground meat again.

"Mommy." Tommy skipped into the kitchen and patted her cheek. "Don't be sad."

Until he said it, she had not realized that tears had been running down her cheeks. She wiped them away with the back of her hand.

Josh stood in the doorway between the kitchen and living areas and stared hard eyes at her, unblinking and defiant.

"Mom," Chloe said, "Josh and I will be back in a little while."

"Can I come?" Tommy asked.

"No, honey. I'm sorry. Mommy needs to talk to Josh alone."

"You're in trouble!" Tommy pumped a fist in the air. Josh never got into trouble.

"Come over here and help Grandma make the Jell-O," Chloe's mom said to Tommy.

A few minutes later, Chloe and Josh parked in town and descended the steps behind city hall to the bike path. They sat on the sand at the water's edge.

Josh hopped in surprise when Chloe sat right down next to the water, her legs in the water, but he sat down next to her without a word.

It was almost dinnertime, and the beach didn't have many people on it. Behind them, Chloe and Josh could hear people on restaurant patios, having cocktails and eating meals and laughing. Chloe didn't know if she'd ever laugh again. Probably, she would. In a year or two.

After a few minutes of sitting, gazing out at the big water that went on for miles, so far that they couldn't see the other side of the lake, Chloe took Josh's small hand in hers.

"I think I know how you feel," she said.

"No, you don't!" He threw her hand from his own and crossed his arms.

"Well, why don't you tell me?"

Josh remained silent.

"Okay. I'll go first. When I left your daddy, I was very sad. We didn't love each other anymore, but we both loved you and Tommy. That won't ever change. That was sad, but we had each other, and Grandma, too. Then my job was gone, but we still had each other. Then Grandma left, and that was really sad because she cooks better than me, but I still had you and Tommy. And Grandma still loved us, she just moved somewhere new. Then…" Chloe took a breath and let the water soothe her.

"Then, someone else left me. Someone I loved very much. And it made me so sad I didn't know how I could walk or talk."

"Luke," Josh said, nodding as if he knew everything that had gone on between Chloe and the Blue Lake bachelor.

He was still staring out over the water, his face serious. She loved that face more than life. She lifted his hair off his forehead and kissed it.

"Not Luke. You, honey. Today, you left me."

She put her arm around her son and hugged him close to her. They cried together and this time she let the tears flow.

"Don't ever leave me again!" she said, after his sobs subsided and he had cried it all out.

"Not even to go to college?"

She laughed, pulling tissues from her purse and handing him one. They both blew their runny noses.

"Okay. You can leave for college. As long as you come home for Christmas."

"And Thanksgiving."

Josh got up and searched the rocky beach for good stones. Good stones, she had learned this week, were the ones that made the biggest splash when you flung them into the water. He threw a few, and then she said dinner was probably ready.

Chloe managed to eat dinner only because Tommy kept his eyes glued to her. He complimented every bite of his grandmother's meal and grinning hard enough to break his face. The smile didn't reach his eyes, which was how she knew he was close to his own meltdown. Unless she could eat the meal, pretend to be okay, be the grownup her boys needed her to be. Still, every bite was a hidden struggle.

Even her normally unflappable mother was quiet during dinner.

Finally, Tommy's fake smile broke. "Why didn't Daddy want Joshua? Doesn't he like us anymore?"

Chapter Eighteen

Chloe sat at the dinner table with her family, trying to think of a good answer to Tommy's question. She had assumed Josh told Tommy why he'd run away. They weren't just brothers, they were also best friends. After the divorce, they were each other's only constant. One day Daddy would be there in the morning or after school to pick them up from the bus stop. Another day Grandma would give them breakfast. Or their mom would tuck them into bed. Sometimes it was hard to remember which grown up would be there when needed, but it was always the two of them, no matter what.

When Josh had left without Tommy today, he had taken a step away from that bond. It had shaken her younger son to the core, she could see now. Of course it had.

She wanted to blurt out her true feelings about the answer to Tommy's questions—that their father was a selfish pig who thought only of his own comfort and pleasure. But was that really the truth? Was she absolutely sure that Spence's motives had been self-serving? Sure, he was an idiot when it came to child psychology, but maybe that was his only mistake.

"It's not that Daddy doesn't want you to live with him. He would give anything in the world to have the two of you every single day of your lives. He said no to

Josh because if he said yes, he'd be breaking the law."

The fib, if that's what it was, came to her in a flash. Earlier the boys had been playing a video game called "Breaking the Law," the object of which was to find as many bad guys as possible and pile them all behind bars.

"Why?" Josh wanted to know.

"What law? The one about stealing or the one about violence?" Tommy quoted from the video game mythology.

"Legally, I have physical custody of you boys. That means if your dad said yes to Josh, he would be breaking the law, and he could go to jail."

That much was true. And who knew? Maybe it had been Spence's true motive, his clumsy response to Josh's cry for help.

While the boys seemed satisfied with her answer, Chloe saddened. Josh had been insecure and anxious under her watch, due to her decisions. She had hurt her child, and she must continue to take actions that would hurt him, and there was not a damn thing she could do to make things different.

"Mommy, if we have to move someplace, let's move here. I like this town." She'd expected Tommy to bring up something like this before. "There's lots of houses for sale here, right, Grandma?"

Her mother got up to pull the bowls of Jell-O from the fridge and busied herself with scooping globs of Cool Whip onto them.

"None for me, Mom. And go easy on the Cool Whip, please."

Her mother made no comment, just set two bowls down before the boys. Apparently, she wasn't that hungry, either.

"Grandma says Daddy's gonna move here and sell houses. And he can show us some. There's one right on this street! Can we, Mom?"

"Can we?" Josh added.

Betrayed and ganged up on, Chloe steeled herself. Every person she knew was blocking her, or trying to, from the sure-thing career Seattle offered. She'd seen the house down the block. It was a darling old red brick house with a big front porch painted white. There was a dormer upstairs and a one-car garage in the back. A part of her yearned to do just as the boys wanted. A large part of her. But she had to be the practical one.

"You know Daddy needs his job, because he has to provide a home and clothes and food for Bettina and your new sister or brother. Those things are very expensive. That's why Mommy needs a good job, too. Because we need a house, and clothes, and food." There was no need to spell out IRA and 401K and college savings accounts to them. "Mommy needs a really good job, a job that's worth two normal jobs. Those jobs are hard to find. But I was lucky. I found one. In Seattle."

"Hard to find like Public Enemy Number One," Tommy said, still thinking along the lines of his video game.

"Well, sort of, except the job is good, and Public Enemy is bad."

"The job is bad! It's making us move away from Grandma and Daddy and our new little sister who might be a brother who is not even born yet!" Josh shoved his Jell-O across the table. The half-eaten bowl landed with a crash on her mother's kitchen floor.

For a minute Josh seemed surprised and even a

little apprehensive about what he'd done, but then he crossed his arms and glared at her, daring her to deny the truth of his words.

"Tell Grandma you're sorry for breaking her bowl," Chloe said, grabbing paper towels and bending to clean up the mess. Her mother stood next to the sink, holding onto the countertop. As Chloe deposited the mess in the trash and rinsed off her hands, another wave of guilt engulfed her. She had done this to all of them. Her mother was getting older. Yes, she'd decided to retire to a more laid-back way of life, but Chloe was doing more than cutting apron strings. She was cutting her mother's heart out.

"Sorry, Grandma," Josh said.

Her mother released the countertop and went over to hug Josh. Tommy finished his Jell-O, his eyes wide.

"We should go," Chloe said. They were leaving Blue Lake in the morning, packing up the car for their cross-country adventure.

"Bonfire!" Tommy said.

Cloe sighed. The boys were now addicted to s'mores. And they surely didn't need any more sugar tonight. But she felt that to deny them small pleasures would just make the big move that much worse.

"Bonfire," she agreed.

While the boys put away their video game, she helped her mother with the dishes. She washed, Mom dried and put away. Chloe hadn't learned where things were placed in her mother's new kitchen yet, and probably never would. A sad sigh escaped before she could swallow it.

"Tommy's right, you know," her mom said while the water ran into the dishpan. "You could find a local job, buy a house here in town. Life is more affordable than you think when you move away from the city. We need less here."

"Oh, Mom." Chloe was close to tears again. And she was not a crier. "I can't live here. Not ever."

"But why not? This is a perfect little town. It has everything we need."

"Luke hates me." It popped out before she knew she'd said it. "Also I know I'll never find a job like the one in Seattle here in farm country. Failing farm country."

"Listen, dear. You can't worry about what he thinks. I'm sorry it didn't work out for you two. I really am. But you'll get over it. And you shouldn't drag your kids across the country because some big lummox broke your heart."

Chloe put an arm around her mother. She knew Ursula understood very well why Chloe wanted to take the job in Seattle. Chloe had told her the income, the bonuses, the matching 401K. She'd described the extent of the health care package. She mentioned the price of a year of college these days. One year for one student. Her mother had been shocked at how college costs had sky-rocketed just since Chloe had finished off her degree.

They both wanted the best for the boys. They both knew the boys would survive and thrive in Seattle. It really wasn't about Luke. His beliefs just strengthened her resolve to leave.

"I'll fly you out every winter. I'll buy a house with a wing just for you. I'll bring the boys back to see their dad as often as I can arrange it. I'll do whatever it takes."

"I know, dear. I know."

Her mother kissed her on the side of her face, right where she always did, between her cheek and her ear. Chloe had missed her mother so much in the few weeks they'd been apart. But she'd be too busy working, proving she was worth her huge salary, to dwell on that once she got to Seattle.

Chapter Nineteen

Luke had seen Chloe and Josh earlier that evening as he was having a beer after work on the back patio of Captain's, which had a lake view. They were at the beach. Things seemed like they had smoothed over since the kid had run away earlier in the day.

He had been trying to forget about Chloe, but she turned up everywhere, if not in person, then in his mother's conversations. As in right now, when she called to ask if he knew Chloe was leaving tomorrow.

Luke sighed. He had not lived with his parents since he graduated from high school. He'd lived first in a rental with two other guys, then the condo with Abby and Bella. After they busted up, he finally bought a house with a huge barn out back where he could store all his equipment. It was an old farmhouse, big and drafty and falling into disrepair. He fixed something when he absolutely had to, so it wasn't a complete shambles anymore, but he still had the odd motor in the kitchen cupboard, hammer and screwdrivers in the cutlery drawer.

Right now, he wanted a clean plate for his steak and baked potato currently burning on the grill. He should have eaten at Captain's. Except the place had been full of tourists, and he'd seen her on the beach and felt like he needed to go home and lick his wounds. Then his mother called. Meanwhile, his dinner blackened on the grill while he searched in vain for a clean plate.

He found something to use as a plate. "You leave a pie tin thing over here?" He took it out of the cupboard and walked out to the backyard. He didn't have a deck even though he built them for other people. Just a lawn chair and a grill. Good enough.

"What? Never mind. Just remember. This is your last chance. She's leaving here tomorrow, leaving the state for good. Don't let her get away, son. I know that if you do, you'll be sorry for a long time. Maybe forever."

"Gotta go. Dinner's gonna burn." He clicked off after telling her he loved her.

He forked the steak and foiled potato into the pie tin and took it back inside. He knew exactly where he kept the steak knives and the A1 sauce. He even had butter for a change.

He sat down to eat his meal. It was so easy to tell his mother he loved her, but he'd only said it once to Chloe. He didn't like admitting how much he loved her, even to himself, because what good would it do? She was not the woman he thought she was when he fell in love with her. He stopped in midchew. Well, damn it, he had fallen in love. He'd been hoping it was just infatuation. Lust. Something simple. But no.

And she was so out of his league. She did city girl things with people and computers that made him feel like a hick country boy. The salary she'd been offered was triple what he made in a year. Of course she was going to take it. She'd be an idiot not to. And then there were the boys. He loved them, too. Sigh. As much as he'd tried to keep them out of his heart, it hadn't happened. He'd broken his number one rule, and now he had to pay the price.

He cut another big piece of meat and shoved it into his mouth. She'd said something about him moving to Seattle. In all the middle of that stuff about her ex. Yeah, he could mow her lawn and clean her pool, maybe some of her neighbors would hire him, too.

He finished his meal and threw the pie tin in the garbage. He didn't feel like doing dishes. He was garbage. Not good enough. He was not an optimistic type to begin with, and he needed positive support to feel halfway decent. His parents and friends provided that support most of the time. Now his mom had gone rogue and probably taken his dad along for the ride.

He turned on the game and popped another beer. But the same thing that had happened in the kitchen occurred in the living room. It didn't matter what room he was in, his mind would not release Chloe and her boys.

What if he'd been wrong about her marriage? What if his experience with Abby had prejudiced him? Maybe Chloe's reason to split was reasonable. Maybe he'd been the unreasonable one. He knew Spence was an ass. Had known it from the day he'd dropped those boys off in the street and taken off without even caring whose pickup was parked in the driveway or if anybody else had been home.

If he really loved her, and around his third beer he came to the reluctant conclusion that probably he did, he should let her go. The boys would have a wonderful life, and Chloe would meet someone else and fall in love and get married, and he'd hear about it all secondhand from his mother.

He went to the fridge for another beer, but he was fresh out. Out of beer, out of luck, out of his mind. Because he was starting to think about how the house would feel with Chloe and the boys in it. And that wasn't going to happen.

Chapter Twenty

Chloe brushed her teeth, put on a nightgown, lay down on the lavender-scented sheets Wanda had insisted on washing and ironing every day, but she didn't sleep. Not for hours. Instead she had one of those hell nights where every mistake she'd ever made came back to haunt her and taunt her. Regrets. Fears. Hurt. Pain. She wished she had one of those sleeping pills with the slyly reassuring names that were endlessly advertised on television. Instead, she settled for a cup of chamomile tea and a dispirited survey of the moon.

At dawn, she woke the boys. Maybe they could sneak out with no good-byes. Josh handed her a map of a route he had plotted across the northern states with a stop at Mt. Rushmore. Both boys were so sleepy, she packed healthy snacks and didn't make them eat any breakfast.

As if guided by internal mom radar, Ursula pulled up just as Chloe settled the boys in the car. They had both rested their heads right down on pillows, and Chloe had been hoping for a few quiet hours of driving. No such luck. Ursula stuck her head in the back seat with hugs and kisses for her grandsons. Who were now awake and alert.

Chloe could swear she saw Luke's truck, camouflaged by the dim breaking of day and the line of trees in the state park lot next door. She didn't stare too long. Everything hurt so much. Her splitting headache, tired eyes, sore heart.

When Spence and Bettina came out of Kiwi cottage, both boys scrambled out of the car and ran to their dad. Spence knelt on one knee to hug and kiss his kids, eyes locked on hers, full of tears he would not let fall. When they hugged her belly, Bettina bawled once, then stuffed it back inside. When Tommy patted her tummy softly and said, "Bye-bye, baby. I love you," Chloe knew what it took for Bettina not to open her mouth and let her sorrow pour out.

They had to get out of this place. Now.

****

From the cab of his truck, Luke watched Chloe and the boys back out of Blue Heaven. None of them noticed him. They were going, they were gone, vanished down the highway. In a burst of clarity, he knew why people sometimes got addicted: the pain was too much and they wanted it to go away.

A knock on his window startled him. Ursula. "Come on in and have a cup of coffee with your mama and me."

He didn't want coffee. He looked toward where Chloe's car had been parked just minutes ago, now there were just Spence and Bettina, holding each other up. With slow steps, he carried his heavy heart to Blue Heaven.

"Coffee, guys?" Ursula called.

Bettina shook her head no and walked to Kiwi cottage. Spence came into the bungalow with them. Luke wished he'd never gotten out of his truck.

"I think she'd come back for you," Spence said. Ursula poured coffee into cups all around.

Spence. Luke wanted to spit at the guy. What the hell did he know? Luke's mother would not like it if he said what he was thinking, so he kept quiet.

"She loves you." Ursula put sugar and cream in her coffee and stirred.

How does she know? He still had nothing he could say out loud.

"Do you love her?" It was his own mother this time. Well, they got what they wanted, but things didn't turn out as planned.

"I do." He shrugged. "All three of them."

"I know it's not my place to say, but I need this family to work," Spence said. "Maybe it sounds stupid, but it seems like, here, we could really do it."

"Huh." Wanda's short huff was the only response Spence got. Luke felt a little twinge for the guy. People didn't ask to be addicts, they were just weak or something. Tommy and Josh had that same DNA. They could become addicts. It was possible. With a single working mom, and tons of spending cash, it was even more possible. Families could be effed up. But here, if they were all here…

"Do you know what a headhunter is?" Ursula asked Luke. He was glad to stop his mind from moving in the direction it had been going. Agree with Spence? A man who had put his wife, hell, two wives, and his children, through hell?

"Uh, secret agents?"

"No." Wanda explained about what Chloe did and how she could do it online. "I'm no dummy. I figured this out and told her about it. I wanted her to stay just like you do. But I couldn't get through to her." Wanda got up, put her coffee cup in the sink, and gripped his shoulder.

"You're going to have to go after her, son. Apologize. Beg. Lay out the Spence plan. They say it takes a village to raise a child. Well, maybe it takes this town to keep a family together."

"She made her choice," Luke said, standing so that Wanda's hand fell from his shoulder. He stomped out the door. Two old busybody women and a basket case of a man were not about to tell him what to do. And yet, when he got to his turn, where he meant to pick up his equipment trailer and get on with today's jobs, he didn't stop. He kept driving. Thinking. She had asked him to go with them to Seattle, but he had not asked her to stay here with him in Blue Lake. He never for a minute thought she would. But he should have at least asked.

He wondered as the miles rolled by. Would she have stayed it he'd only asked her? What made him so afraid to hear the word no? Because it would kill him. Not literally, but he'd be dead inside. He was a one-woman man, and Chloe was the one. His car headed down the highway, following the only woman who mattered to him. He loved her a thousand times more than he had realized only an hour ago when he'd sat like a coward and watched her and the boys leave his life forever.

He could have at least put up a fight. Made a counter-offer. Hell, if she'd still have him, he'd accept hers. He didn't want to. Seattle would suck so bad. But if it that was the only card on the table, he'd take it.

****

Chloe made it to Muskegon early in the afternoon. The boys had cried for a solid hour and then fallen asleep for two more. She distracted them with a fast food lunch, healthy snacks untouched, while Josh explained to Tommy that they were going to drive their car onto a big boat and it would take them to another state.

"Oh, Seattle?"

"No, dummy, we still have to go through Wisconsin, Minnesota, North Dakota, Montana, and Idaho. Then we'll be in Seattle."

"Mom, is he telling the truth?" Tommy didn't mention that Josh had called him a dummy.

Chloe nodded, eyes on the road. The distance was ridiculous. Why did she decide to drive? She could have had her car shipped, taken the boys on their first air flight. They could have gotten those little wing pins. Did airlines still give those out? Her neck hurt from continuously peeking in the rearview mirror to check on the boys and then back at the road ahead. "Josh. My phone is dead. Can you plug it in?"

"Not with my seat belt on," Josh said with a fake smile on his face. She had a feeling he was going to hate her for a while.

She pulled into the next rest area they came to and connected the charger to her phone. "Anybody want a candy bar?" She knew bribing them with chicken nugget lunches, soda, chips and candy couldn't be good, but this drive was so much worse than she imagined. She berated herself again. Why hadn't they flown? They didn't have a ton of luggage. She'd planned to buy pretty much everything new. New life, new clothes, new house. Why did she want to cry?

She wanted her mom. So strange. They'd lived in each other's pockets for a long time; she'd taken it all for granted. Now she knew the rip of kin from kin, and it hurt.

Instead of a candy bar, Tommy wailed that he wanted to go home. Josh turned his face into his elbow and wept silently.

All at once she knew that the physical pain inside her was what her boys felt, but theirs worse, because they'd lost their dad, too.

She'd never really had Luke to lose. She couldn't blame him for any of this agony, but she still did.

Finally, they were heading toward the ferry on Lakeshore Drive. There was the water. The enormous sleek boat. There were the five lanes, three to drive aboard, two for departing. She slotted her car into the queue.

When they saw cars pulling onto the ferry, both boys began screaming. They were terrified, tired, and sugared out. Her ears rang, and she put her car in park, since the line was not moving, not at all, and put her hands over her ears. "Please stop." Near tears herself, the last thing these boys needed now was for their mom to break down. The line finally moved an inch, so she crept forward. This was far more difficult than she'd ever imagined.

"Mommy, please don't do it. What if the boat sinks? Those cars weigh a lot and all the people, too, we might drown."

At least they'd stopped screaming, but their whimpers broke her heart. She explained that this ferry was specially built, that it crossed over to Wisconsin several times a day, every day, and it never sank. Ever.

****

Luke pulled into Muskegon and found Lakeshore Drive. He spotted Chloe's car, next to board. He looked around for a place to park. Full public lot, roadside curbs jammed tight with parked cars. Tourist season on this side of the state was just as busy as on their side. He had no way to get to her except through the outgoing ferry lanes, which were empty. But what if a vehicle did depart? And he crashed? Should he try her cell again? The last time he'd called her, the phone had gone directly to voice mail. She'd likely seen his name and didn't pick up.

She was angry. He'd been cruel. She didn't trust him anymore. Probably excited about starting her new life, not thinking about him at all.

What was he doing here anyway? He'd traveled all this way, and he hadn't planned any speech. Oh, God, a dock worker waved her onto the ferry. Without thinking, he sped through the exit lanes and stopped at an angle next to her. Ten guys in fluorescent vests with big flashlights rushed toward them. Angry drivers blasted their horns. Luke opened the door of his truck just as the cops pulled up, sirens wailing, behind him. He got out of his truck.

The boys turned their heads and went wild with joy when they saw him. They ran from the car to him just as a cop and a ship person approached. The boys each grabbed one of Luke's denim legs.

"Please don't arrest him, ocifer," Tommy begged.

"Officer," Josh corrected. "We can explain."

Luke turned from the boys to the cop to that first car in the ferry line being instructed to turn out of the double line full of holiday-types. Every car backed up a few inches so Chloe could accomplish this. Lots of kids, and a few grown-ups, had their heads out windows, rubbernecking.

Chloe drove as directed, headed away from the ferry. Many gesturing officials made it obvious that she had been made to do this, and without the boys. They all three waved at her and Luke gave her a thumbs up. Meanwhile, the ferry people and policemen conferenced while one officer asked for his license and registration. "Have you been drinking, sir?"

"No. I...there was nowhere to park. I need her—" The ferryman once again motioned Chloe to turn out into the street. A police officer—man, there were three cars here, slow day in Muskegon—waved her on. Not letting her stop. He was adamant. He didn't know Chloe. She stopped in the middle of traffic and got out of the car.

****

Chloe started to head toward her boys, but an officer stepped up to her and told her to move her vehicle or be towed. "Those are my boys over there."

The officer looked to where Luke and the boys waved. Luke had a ticket in his hand. His face had a huge smile covering it anyway. "We can do two things, ma'am. One, I can escort your sons over to you, or two, you can leave them with their dad until you find a place to park."

"Oh, he's not their dad." She blushed. She wished he was their dad. And he'd come. Had he changed his mind? Would he travel with them to Seattle after all?

****

"Officer, she's moving across the country, and I've driven clear across this state just to beg her not to go. I know I've broken a few rules. If you just let me bring the boys to her—"

The cops gestured to each other and to the

206

enthralled crowd. "Here's what we're going to do," the officer told Luke.

"Buddy, you can't leave your car there like that," a loudmouthed buttinski driver yelled, honking a long, constant tone. Anger came off the cars in the queue in waves, just like the hot sun.

Luke rubbed the boys' heads. "No problem. We'll sort this out."

Chloe turned back to her car. She got in. His heart fell to the bottom of the harbor. Then the boys were jumping up and down beside him, talking excitedly, explaining to the police officer that Luke was their friend and he was only trying to find them and bring them home. The frazzled cop kept the boys with him while directing Luke to back out of the illegal parking spot.

The cop pointed to a shady spot with grass, well out of the ferry traffic, where the boys should sit.

"Are we going to jail?" Tommy began to cry. "We weren't breaking the law."

"Yeah," Josh said, "explain what law we broke and why we can't go with our Mom. Or Luke." When Luke heard this typical big brother defense, he wondered how he ever thought he could live without these three people. His people.

Some complicated shifting went on with the vehicles and even as the line began to move again some guy flashed Luke his middle finger. "Wait for me!" he yelled to the boys. He carefully backed, then drove ahead, slowly. At an ice cream shop, a car pulled out. He pulled in, parked, and grabbed his keys.

He headed back to the harbor, but saw Chloe's car there in the road right beside him, the boys safely tucked in the back seat. She smiled at him.

****

There wasn't another parking spot, and Chloe couldn't stop traffic again, not with all the police around. But the congested street made the boys beg to get out and go to Luke at the ice cream stand, so she stopped just long enough for them to hop out. Luke was there at the car door and scooped them up, one in each arm.

Chloe's eyes locked with Luke's for a minute until the horns started up again. He would know she was coming back. She'd left her most precious collateral. It took two turns around the long block before she found a spot to park. Then she stopped the car, pocketed her keys, and took off at a run to find Luke. Why was he here? What could it mean? Had something happened to her mom? To Bettina and the baby? Or was it the other thought? Her first thought? He was here for them.

When she got to the ice cream shop, the boys were already licking cones, their sweet faces turned up toward the sunshine. Luke saw her and smiled. He didn't run to meet her, but stood guard over the boys.

She flipped her sunglasses up, all her questions in her eyes. Then she was in his arms.

"I can't let you go," he said.

"I don't want to go." She put her head down on his shoulder and rested in the comfort of his arms.

He hugged her tighter. "What about that fancy job waiting in Seattle?"

"It's too far away." She lifted her face, and he kissed her right there in front of the ice cream stand. When she opened her eyes, the boys were bumping fists and slurping melting ice cream. Her heart slowed and she stayed in Luke's embrace, grateful and amazed that he had found them.

An interview with Cynthia Harrison

1. You said that your husband gave you the idea for this book twenty-five years ago. Why didn't you write your true love story?

I'm a fiction writer. I like making things up. I also wanted to protect the privacy of the real people involved in this story. Not just my husband and sons, but their father, their other mother, and their siblings.

2. Their other mother? Why not stepmom? Do you mean the character of Bettina?

I've always felt, from almost the first day, great respect for the woman who would help raise my children. I feel like I can talk to her about anything and she will understand. She's very friendly and open and nonjudgmental. I love her. She took great care of my children; she is truly their other mother. Stepmom has such negative connotations in literature. She's the opposite of that.

3. So the next obvious question is your ex-husband. Is he anything at all like Spence?

Not an iota. Not even close. Spence is the character I had the most trouble with, at first. I didn't want to make the ex the bad guy. It's such a cliché. So I did the opposite and that didn't work. This is fiction, and I needed conflict. I'm a writer who teaches, and the first seven years of my teaching career, I taught at-risk high school children. I learned a lot about addictions and how they destroy families. Then there's my addiction to chocolate and potato chips, which sounds funny but created serious consequences. I was recently diagnosed with pre-diabetes. So no more sugar for me. I have an addictive personality. Fortunately, I can't drink more than a few glasses of wine without getting dizzy and then sick. So food has been my primary addiction, but I am also a binge television watcher, huge movie fan, and constant reader of novels. Aside from the food, these are all soft addictions, but they all gave me insight into Spence.

4. What will happen to Spence? Will he be okay? How can the reader know?

As a reader, I sometimes have questions when a story ends, too. In the literature, the relapse number is very high, but Spence has a unique supportive system in Blue Lake. We will see Spence in other stories, but I don't know if he will relapse because he hasn't (yet). Still, it's true what they say: addicts will always be in recovery.

5. How many books do you plan for the Blue Lake Series?

I still have a lot of stories to tell. I like telling two thematically related stories in every novel. So Fast Eddie's will be about the reunion of Bob and Lily, who were going off to college in Blue Heaven. They've graduated, and Lily comes back to Blue Lake. So does Eddie's first love. My favorite way to write is to have a new adult storyline and a more mature romance as well.

6. *Blue Heaven* was more of a traditional romance, but *Luke's #1 Rule* had many more characters. There are the four adults and two children, plus the meddling mothers. Why the change?

They say every writer has a "book of her heart." Luke's Number #1 Rule was mine. It was not just a love story, although that's the main plotline. Using the theme of blending a family was the book I've always wanted to write. It was a challenge. And it wasn't a romance. I will always write love stories because I have a romantic soul, but the larger picture interests me, too.

7. You said you're a reader. Who are some of your favorite authors?

If you came to my house, you would look at my bookshelves and know. I use an e-reader these days, but still collect my favorites in hardback. First came Jane Austen and Erica Jong, then Alice Hoffman, Louise Erdrich, Sara Lewis, Elizabeth Berg. I also love poetry and short stories, so add Margaret Atwood and Alice Munro. Also Carol Shields.

8. Do you read male authors?

I do. Raymond Carver is a personal favorite. I also admire TC Boyle and Richard Ford. There is not a book by David Lodge I have not laughed through. Richard Russo is in there, too. I don't collect any of them except Carver. I think taking two degrees in English literature filled me up with male authors. The classics. After college, I started my own education of contemporary female writers.

9. Do you read contemporary romance?

I do. I never miss a novel by Barbara Delinsky, Pamela Morsi, or Rachel Gibson. I'm also a fan of romantic suspense and several of my fellow TWRP authors write in that line. Mysteries! Sue Grafton and Anne Perry. Lee Childs. Every book.

10. How do you find the time to teach, read, and write? Are your little boys grown up now?

Yes, my boys are grown with families of their own. When they were young, I wrote less and read less. I enjoyed my time with them. More recently, I've been teaching less, which gives me time to read and write. I've found you can do it all, but you can't do it all at the same time. I'm also dedicated (again, I could say addicted) to Twitter and my blog. My older son suggested I start a blog in 2002. He set it up for me, and I'm still there at www.cynthiaharrison.com. For ten years, I wrote about my efforts to publish my novels. Then it happened and I decided to write about other things, the concerns in my novels, but also the love and joy in everyday life.

11. Do you ever speak to book clubs?

I adore meeting people I've only known on the Internet. In real life, I've met friends from New York, San Diego, Los Angeles, and Seattle. I live north of Detroit, but, time permitting, I'd be happy to Skype with a book group from anywhere in the world. One of my favorite things to do is talk books.

Book Group Discussion Questions
for *Luke's #1 Rule*

1. Are the choices Chloe makes based on her own needs or the needs of her children? Why?
2. Is Luke's love for Chloe in question because he will not move away with her?
3. Do the mothers meddle too much?
4. How much is too much when it comes to sticking with a substance abusing spouse? Should Bettina cut her losses or give Spence one more chance?
5. Chloe earns much more, or has the potential to do so, than Luke. Does she owe it to her children to secure a financially sound future above true love?
6. Is Blue Lake the right place for all of these people to be? Does close community help heal families?
7. Blending families needs a delicate touch. Are there things Chloe could have done differently?
8. Will Spence ever get his act together? Will it stick? Why or why not?

A word about the author...

Cynthia Harrison teaches writing to college students, including creative writing. Cindy has blogged at www.cynthiaharrison.com since 2002. She has two previous novels with The Wild Rose Press, *The Paris Notebook* and *Blue Heaven*. *Blue Heaven* is the first of her six-book Blue Lake series. She loves talking books with readers and welcomes book club discussions in person or online. Her exclusive interview about the themes of divorce, single parenthood, blending families, and addiction is live on her website.

~*~

Three time award winner for:
Your Words, Your Story (writing manual);
Snow Day (short memoir);
Africa (poem).

~*~

**Other Cynthia Harrison titles
available from The Wild Rose Press, Inc.:**
BLUE HEAVEN (Blue Lake Series)
THE PARIS NOTEBOOK

~*~

BLUE HEAVEN is a best seller
on Amazon Free List
#1romance
#1women's fiction
#1contemporary fiction